Exiles
By
Jay T Wright

CW00386386

Published by Underground Assembled
Copyright 2020
Cover 'Alexandria' by Jay Wright
Library of Congress Number: 2023902557

1.

In the sunset, a whooping drunken hollering followed by a fist connecting through bushy beard. Rows of dilapidated mobile homes hunker against the edge of the white and brown mottled desert.

A lone figure sits in a chipped lawn chair which leans slightly, the checkered webbing frayed. His beard is slightly unkempt. He wears oversized boots caked in mud, and a long dirty coat wrapping around stubby legs. Fake blue fur lines the coat. Encrusted in it is the dirt of the desert. He wears dark welding goggles, and doesn't seem to have noticed the end of the day.

More drunken whooping and hollering. Figures of his fellow workers in front of him in the dusk, wrestling, drinking, throwing the odd empty bottle. Another thrown fist. "Hey." One of them stumbles backwards avoiding the flailing lunatic who threw the punch in the middle of a harmless alcohol soaked wrestling match. He trips over his own feet and falls backwards against one of the trailer homes. He knocks over pickaxes and shovels that lean haphazardly.

Miners.

Tartus rolls his eyes, and puts the goggles on his forehead, a headache settling over him. He looks up at the hooligans from the ratty lawn chair, depressed.

Tihan says,"Tartus, come on, it was a long day."

The goggled figure exuding black mood and irritation looks their way, but doesn't move.

"We start swing next week. Come on; let them off the rock breaking detail."

"Nights? Now we complain about working in the dark?" asks Tartus.

"We dig because we dig digging. Dark. Light. Depth. Water. Gas, of any kind," and here the miner, Tarnus, who threw the punch reaches in his pants, spreads an ass cheek, and farts dramatically," nothing stops us."

Tartus making an affirmative gesture again, this time even more grimly.

"We go out tonight, we find weak ale, depilated women, and trouble," Tarnus says,"We get in a fight, we get bruised, we wake up with aches tomorrow morning and everything seems better."

"And we're poorer," Tartus adds. "It's not like we're digging for gold out here."

"True."

"If only we were," says Tihan. Whooping assent from the group of miners.

Trying to cheer up Tartus, Tarnus shouts at battle cry level,

"We dug almost to the old country today, we must... GET DRUNK!"

Tartus says,"You are drunk." Then adds,"And keep it down someone will hear you."

Tarnus shouts,"DRUNKER!" The group cheers.

Tihan chimes in,"Prepare the steed!" Tihan grabs Tartus and pulls him grudgingly out of the chair.


2.


The dark pyramid reflects the airport, the desert, the strip twinkling below, the stars above, and the dark sky. The black pyramid holding its secrets close. A light in an angled window of the black glass pyramid, where someone tall and thin stands, watching planes half a mile away climb into the sky, or swoop like giant birds to claw tarmac. The blue glow of jet exhaust stark against the night. He stands, nearly as tall as the window, hypnotized by the comings and goings of the planes. Metal birds nearly mystical against the strange constellations. Unmarked ones headed for the deep desert. Others going to places far away he can barely imagine, even though he sees a likeness of them here every day. Like when something is not the real thing.

Behind him three women sleep in various states of undress on a sumptuous oversized bed. Figures of different ancients than he has known surround them. Plaster, not stone. The sound of running water from the foyer. He can't remember which one of the women he had first or what their names are; practically anything about them. They started in the pool of running water in the main room, and progressed into the bedroom. They have barely registered on him, a tiny blip in a long life. He feels so old, and it takes so much to break through that now.

He met them down on the strip. The vintage Italian V6 purred along. He was checking his cell phone for messages. He had stopped the red supercar at a stoplight. He had the windows down, listening to some local music.

The three attractive women had pulled up next to him in something in German silver.

Fenur said,"Formal salutations and... Excuse me, ladies?"

The women looked over, then their driver's side window slid down.

The driver, a redhead, he knows as a magical kind of good luck said,"Yes?"

"Formal salutations and goodwill," which they met with laughter,"Would you care to meet me for a foray into later?" Fenur asked. He threw them each a thousand dollar chip from the casino expertly through the window. "You see, I have these extra chips, and I have no idea how to get rid of them; I was wondering if you could assist me?"

The blonde in the passenger seat started to say,"We were-"

The redhead cut her off "-We might be over that way later." Always good luck.

"You will find me at the tropical scenery bar in the hotel, and if you don't see me ask for me by my given name Fenur. Most excellent, and formal goodbyes!" He stepped on the gas, sending the vintage sports car off through the intersection, the light having turned green ages ago.

Fenur puts on his tuxedo quietly, trying not to wake the three. He smiles to himself. In the alcove where he had laid his clothes, where the sinks and the mirror are, he catches his reflection. He has an eye for detail. He stops and stands in front of the mirror. A gray hair. He has a gray hair. He frowns, grabs it nimbly and pulls. Stares at it. Throws it away.

Back in the main room, he crosses towards the door.

One of the women wakes slightly. The passenger. The blonde.

"Hey," she says.

"Yes?" he asks her.

"What is it exactly you do?" she looks up at him sleepily, still holding onto her friends' arm which drapes over her.

"Me?" he says slyly, leaning down next to her, and petting her head. "Not as much as I used to. Rest well, young one."

She closes her eyes, snuggling in against her friend who tightens her grip slightly.

He rises and heads for the door.


## 3.


The steed is a rattling, beat up, rusting-out LRII complete with safari package, circa dawn of history. It rumbles through the orange and pink flickering glow of the Las Vegas strip.

Tihan mumbling,"Local piss water; not much likelihood of getting truly drunk."

The LRII backfires.

"Careful, one of us has to stay sober to drive this contraption. I mean, is alcohol and hairless girls all you think about?" Tartus asks from behind the welding goggles.

"Not much else to think about around these parts." Tihan honks the LRII's horn and swerves lightly around a jaywalker.

"Run!" shouts Tarnus out the open roll cage at the still living but quickly fleeing tourist. "These desert dwellers are cowards, all of them. Look at the way they run from a real machine, from real workers. Digging. Digging for what? For who? For us? HAH! Little holes in the ground is all we dig here. Little hidey-holes for something that - what? It's not even WORTH ANYTHING!"

"We are what we dig," grumbles Tartus.

"Then we are worthless," says Tihan.

The LRII turns off the strip, rumbles through an alley and over a sidewalk, a half-mown urban meadow full of rotting fast food containers and broken bottles, up and over curb stops in a parking lot by force of live axle and four wheel drive, sets off car alarms on econoboxes and customs alike, makes a u-turn and parks across three parking spots at the back of the lot. It dies in a great gout of oil smoke.

The crew of miners jumps down from the height of the LRII and regroups in front of Love Jonze, the club emanating a deep throbbing and portentous sound.

The sound is a deafening throaty roar inside. They pass through a metal detector unhindered. It sounds like the furnaces from the mines. It sounds like what powered the furnaces.

Past the metal detector a bouncer who remembers them.

"Hey, back again I see," says the bouncer as they walk through the door.

"Yeah," says Tarnus, stopping and turning on the gigantic man.

"You pretty brave for a little man," says the bouncer. "Good thing we don't have a marker next to the door, says you have to be this tall to ride the girls." The bouncer laughs behind his hand, not bothering to even rise from his stool.

Tihan takes Tarnus by the arm, and pulls on him. The bouncer continues laughing as Tarnus allows himself to be pulled away.

"Can we get this over with?" asks Tartus.

As they lose sight of the bouncer in the crowd of taller people Tarnus cheers up. "If these wenches can't move you from your trolllike state, Tartus, I despair for you," he says.

The three sit at the bar of the strip club Love Jonze watching wistfully as stilletoe shoes clack in front of them on a mirror.

"What about this was going to change my mind?" asks Tartus.

"He's a deviant, Tarn. A good old-fashioned hair-pulling rugburner. You're after my own heart." Tartus looks sideways towards Tihan at this. "Can't tell in the dark of a mine, can you, Tar?" asks Tihan.

"Tihan, I will never be that desperate," responds Tartus.

"You never know."

"Why do you call me Tar and him Tarn? You could just call us both Tar if you're that desperate to save milliseconds of time."

"That would be confusing." "More confusing than calling us by half our name?" "Here we go again..." interjects Tarnus.

"It's just a figure of speech," says Tihan defensively.

"It's a locals' figure of speech."

A moment while Tihan considers continuing to argue. Decides against it. "Have some more of this, whatever it is. I hesitate to call it ale," she says and pushes a half-full bottle in front of him.

Tihan signals for another round, which appears immediately.

Tartus looks down at the new beer, up at the naked woman in front of him, gets up, and heads for the door.

"Come on, Tihan was only joking, Tar..." At the door the bouncer taunts,"Thanks, come again".

Tartus stops. "YOU WILL DIE WITH MY AXE THROUGH YOUR SKULL."

"Bring it, little man."

Having had enough, Tartus grabs the bouncer by the balls and lifts him into the air, shoving him against the mirrored glass wall of the club next to the exit. The bouncer howls. Tartus punches him with his free arm while the bouncer struggles.

He drops the bouncer who curls into a ball on the grubby, sticky floor.

Tihan following. The owner and bartender out of an office doorway in the back, over a countertop; the owner with a chromeplated .45 and the bartender with a shotgun. Semi-nude girls sway uncertainly on high heels and clamber down off the runway to hide behind it, the music coming to a sudden stop.

Axes drop out of long dirty coats. Shiny and engraved they reflect the low light of the club, completely different from the digging tools they had propped against the mobile home after work.

"Tiny?" shouts the owner.

"I'm alright," the bouncer whimpers.

"You, you and you. All you short guys stay where you are," says the owner menacingly.

"Or what?" asks Tartus. The owner waves the chrome-plated .45. "See the big gun?"

"Oh, I thought you meant something serious."

Tartus throws the axe. It makes sharp zing sound as it slices through metal rips the gun from the hand of the owner. Two pieces fall to the floor.

The bartender, who was not exactly backing up the owner before, hold the shotgun away, putting it down on the ground. The bartender says,"Guys we don't want any trouble. Ok? We have plenty of money-"

"You. Stow it." Points at Tarnus. "Pick up my axe. And we have enough money, fool," he says, turning his back on all of them.

Tartus makes it to the door, past the bouncer and out on to the street.

Tihan follows him out.

"Come on, Tar. Come back. We'll give them some money; it will be alright I'll buy you a lapdance..." Tihan says.

"Why? For what? From one of those? THEY LOOK LIKE THE ALBINO BLIND FISH WE USED TO FIND WRIGGLING AROUND AT THE BOTTOM OF THE MINE SHAFTS WHEN THEY FILLED UP WITH WATER!" Tartus keeps walking. "And you!" He points at Tarnus, turning around for a second and walking backwards. "You better have my good axe!"

"Come on, man. It's not that bad. They're kind of nice once you get used to it-" Tihan offers.

"...you would say that, Ti..." Tarnus accepting of Tihan's desires but still exasperated with both of them. "It'll be light in a few hours and we have to be back for the dig. Why don't we just stay in the city?" Tarnus hands Tartus back the axe.

"Dig? What dig, MAN?" he spits the word at Tarnus. "You said it yourself: This is NO DIG! For what? For these pasty fools? For us?"

Tarnus puts a hand on Tartus's shoulder.

Tartus slaps it away.

Tarnus jumps on Tartus. Tihan tries to break it up. The three fall to the ground, in a ball of fur, burlap, dust and hair.

A police searchlight falls on the spot where they are wrestling around, throwing ineffective punches at each other.

Sirens, flashing lights.

The three spring up, running.

The police seeing the scattering little people, get out of the car. One follows Tihan across the street, into an alleyway.

The other follows Tarnus into the parking lot. Tartus runs down the street into traffic. The side street comes to a halt as traffic off of the strip immediately begins to pile up, trying to get around the police car.

In the parking lot, the LRII roars back to life, Tarnus behind the wheel. Crunch of the dogbox engaging.

In the alley, Tihan stops and turns realizing there's nowhere to go: the alley has no exit. "Hey." The police flashlight turns, nearly on top of her. The officer gets an eyeful of furry chest and breasts.

He recoils and screams.

"You know you want it."

She pulls the flashlight out of the cop's surprised hand, chucking it onto a roof, and takes off past him, under his arm's reach.

The LRII turns out onto the street, blasting past the other LVPD uniform who is shining a flashlight under cars. Tihan grabs a roll cage bar and pulls herself up into the back driver's side passenger seat.

Further down the road they see Tartus running, axe once more in hand, people scattering out of his way.

"Come on, get in," says Tarnus from the driver's seat.

Tartus climbs sullenly into the passenger seat of the LRII without it stopping.

He looks at the axe before he sheaths it. It has a nick in it.

He holds it up to the other two.

"That's just..."

"What?"

"It has a nick in it."

"It's made of pure nurbinium." "I know. This was my father's axe and his father's before him.

All the way back to before the line of Tar, when we broke from under the mountains. It's worth more than..." He stops, suddenly very serious. "I mustn't think that way."

"Worth more than all of Vegas," Tarnus says. "Worth more than everything they have ever dug out of the ground in these parts. I'm sorry Tartus. Really truly sorry."

4.

In an elevator, Fenur turns his back on the Vegas skyline. He examines his reflection, straightens his tuxedo.

The floor of the dark pyramid has become old Vegas. A place where nothing lasts, the irony of which is not lost on Fenur.

He walks across the floor.

"Sir," one of the bellhops runs up next to him.

"Yes?" he asks.

"The concierge for you, Sir."

Fenur takes a folded twenty dollar bill out and hands it to the bellhop, who accompanies him back to the concierge desk, open even at this late hour. He tries again to fathom why he enjoys working swing. He sighs, it's because he was a child of night.

"Sir," says the woman behind the counter,"This came for you earlier. It was hand delivered by a tall man wearing livery from ... the other side of the strip. The far end. She puts a small wooden lattice crate on the counter. The lattices contain twelve bottles of reddish, black fluid. He stares at the bottles dumbfounded.

"This came from...?" The concierge gestures with her eyes towards the distance.

"Thank you. Please hold on to them for now?" he places another twenty on the counter, which the concierge pockets. "Better: put them in my room."

"Our pleasure, Sir."

Despite everything, new paint, carpets, years now of no smoking in the hotel, he can still smell the smoke. He wonders if the tourists can.

The smell reminds him of the revolt.

Out on the street he walks northeast along the strip towards where he works. The pendants of the fake castle flapping lazily in the high-powered spots in the Vegas night. He likes the way the traffic sounds at night and the play of light here more than over on Fremont Street. He was a child of night; it's why he works swing. How could he forget? There's space outside on the strip. If he stays inside too much the hotels start to get claustrophobic. This kind of meditation clears his head before work. It's his only time alone. Everyone local drives, and tourists take the inter-hotel bus system or the tram. The likelihood he would see anyone else, from either camp, is remote. The heat took adjusting to, but now he can't imagine going back. He used to dream about returning a hero.

He crosses into the pickup and departure area, feels the waves of disappointment mixed with a few bright spots of excitement. Inside the hotel he smells the smell of piped in flowers, not real ones. They keep real ones up front, but they put the smell of flowers into the central air, and sprinkle the rest of the hotel with ornamental flowers made of silk. He isn't sure about the oxygen rumor. If they do he can't feel it; but it's not the sort of thing he would notice. Little things like heat and cold, or thinness of air never affected him much.

He crosses the darkened lobby to a door to a restricted area, shows a security guard he doesn't recognize his identicard. Out of the public area of the hotel, there is no ornamentation. He walks down vague uneasy cement hallways to a locker room area. His coworkers wonder why he always arrives already in his tux. He spent nearly six thousand dollars on the designer label, and he doesn't trust those around him enough to leave it in the locker, whether or not he believes they can break through his locking system.

Inside the locker are his tools, his daily ritual. He rubs his hands in essential oil, notices how low the bottle is getting, puts the bottle away and relocks the locker. He takes a small sculpted piece of metal jewelry he wears around his neck and places it in the locker. After the jewelry is off the lights seem slightly brighter, and a moment of hyper-reality passes over Fenur. He clocks in, and heads back out onto the floor.

On the floor, the floor manager gives him a subtle signal and he walks to a blackjack table where chips are piling up in front of what the floor managers refer to as 'rubes'. He relieves the dealer on duty and takes over, reaching under the green and retrieving fresh cards, cutting them to his own liking.

The floor manager takes the old cards Fenur has laid next to him. The tourists watch Fenur's hands, the cards blurring, shuffling. Adept overly long fingers find the spaced ridges of the cards. Probability and numbers, fingers over the individual ridges in the pack. They put him on a carpeted box that is bolted to the floor, it supposedly gives the dealer command of the table when people are sitting; Fenur hunches to hide his height and still he looms menacingly over the out-of-towners.

Fenur cuts the cards and deals. A moment later he says,"Dealer wins."

Tourists doubling down. Chips rearranged, card player tells he never watches; he just doesn't care. It's like systems: they don't work.

"Dealer wins."

The floor manager has abandoned him knowing the likelihood of a winner at his table.

Again the marks count into the deck, fold, wait, return to the game in the next round. Again,"Dealer wins."

In an hour, the people at the table are openly angry. It's like this every night.

"What the-?" says one of the tourists looking around the table for confirmation.

Another says,"We haven't won all night, man. What is this?"

The one with the system and the tells, or maybe it's the system of tells says,"Come on guys, there are plenty of places on the strip that aren't rigged."

Fenur smiles. "We thank you for your business." Later the floor manager comes up and relieves him.

Fenur walks back to the changing area, near the hotel's offices. In a cubby hole near Fenur's locker lies a check. Fenur takes the check.

"Don't spend it all in one place," says the floor manager ironically, in the middle of changing into a sweatshirt and jeans.

Fenur smiles.

The floor manager continues,"I don't get it, Fee. Why are you still working here? You're good enough to go pro - man, you might as well be. You don't need the money. Why are you hanging out with us lowly mortals? Especially here at a tourist trap."

"Just staying out of view." He puts the sculpted piece of jewelry around his neck again. "I like working here. I like the people I meet."

"You like the tourists? What're you? Joking? You run into some connected guys or something?-" jokes the man, and Fenur laughs "–Yeah, I know, local bogeymen, but it happens.

"You got the looks. You could be on one of those television shows with those looks. Poker night. Play famous people. Endorsements. You could have it all."

"In my experience, Randy, no matter what you have, there's always something else you don't."

"Don't tell me you're happy..."

"No, I wouldn't go that far," says Fenur as he walks out feeling more rattled than he should. He pockets the check.

Outside of her office he can hear shouting. The door to her office slams open and a self-important official looking man in a suit pushes past him, followed by another. He watches the men exit into the lobby of the office.

The second one turns and says,"You will be hearing from the gaming commission on these matters. Jack?"

"I don't think there's anything I can add," says the first man.

He looks at Fenur and scoffs.

"Scasey?" Leanor barks. The first man looks at her, cutting a menacing figure in the hallway just past Fenur. "Any further contact should be through the hotel's lawyers. You are not welcome on the premises again."

"Are you threatening an FBI agent?" asks the gaming commissioner, incredulous. Scasey shakes his head next to the short and portly state gaming regulator.

"No. I'm stating our legal rights," she says flatly.

"We go where we want, when we want," Scasey returns.

"Then we – I personally if necessary - will file for a restraining order." Her skin molten, gusts of breath coming hard. Fenur remembering why he was attracted to her. "Get out!" she adds.

Turning to him she asks,"Fenur?" holding the door for him, which he looks at – probably an obvious gaffe to Leanor. The two men do not notice.

The men board Leanor's private elevator in the reception area.

Fenur walks into Leanor's office.

Leanor stands, seeming rattled. Small things, most people wouldn't notice. Years of association with her leaves her open to him despite her face and even her eyes revealing less than they once did to most of those around her. This concern for her irks him. Behind her a floor to ceiling window in her penthouse office. A tall lanky woman with dark hair and deep sprays of freckles. Through the window the city of indeterminate age. She keeps her desk in front of her the power position in office politics and something Fenur deigns not to notice. A telescope at the window – still some signs of the old ways.

"Thank you for coming," she says, but somehow it sounds ungracious. She gestures to enter but not to sit, slowly she is regaining her composure. To most she would seem unflappable even after the furor he just heard.

"It was hard to miss your message." Fenur sits in one of the oversized green club chairs. He notices it's real leather. The office quiet and well-insulated; even Fenur's hearing can't pick up exterior noise through the air vents, or the throb of people through the floor of the slightly swaying building.

"Was it?" Leanor asks, seeming brisk. She stops. "What are you speaking of?"

"Do you deny you sent it?" he rejoins.

"Sent...?" she seems again as close to flustered as she ever becomes.

"You sent over a crate of dark mead. You wanted my attention – here I am."

Looking at the door Leanor says,"Sent...? Would you believe me if I said I didn't? Fenur, please; not right now."

"Whenever would be a good time?" he asks, not finding her answer credible.

"Those were local officials, I barely understood what they were talking about... Fenur, I didn't send it. Regardless of what others might want you to think."

"I like it - how did you find my quarters over there?"

"With the tourists?"

"No one harries me."

"You think locating that machine of your's is difficult? Or where it spends its nights tethered?"

"It's not a horse. So you left me dark mead?"

"It has a horse on the side doesn't it? You think they had any idea what that gift was at the concierge?" She seems to think this funny.

"No. So you admit sending it?"

"No. I did not send it. A watcher saw you picking it up from the concierge and sent word. Please – this really isn't a good time."

Darkly, he asks,"Why? Why would someone leave me something so... so obscene?"

Leanor waves away this bit of drama. Still looking at the door, she finally refocuses on him. "Fenur, you are no longer indentured to the house of Nor. But you cannot live like this. One of our watchers noted that you had removed your pendant of life." She stares at him over the desk, steeples fingers that are even longer than his, taps them together delicately.

"Your watchers?" he prompts.

"The house has need of such things."

"Are you indenturing locals?"

"Indenturing is such a harsh word." She smiles at this joke she knows he won't think is funny.

Surprised, he asks,"How do they remember between times what you want or need? There was a time-"

"Times are changing, young Fenur. No – we use the younger ones amongst the houses. They are lay-abouts if not given responsibilities."

"Apparently." Fenur explains sharply,"Your house gave me the pendant. I did not always live like houses of Vil or Nor. But it does make it easier. I will wear it if I choose, or not." Fenur contemplates,"Even among the houses – who would leave me dark mead as a gift?"

She laughs softly behind her desk, props a perfect leg up on the dark wood. "Someone who knows how close you are with the clans."

"That would be everyone. Once you would have thought such an item an abomination," he says about the wood desk. Her smile abruptly fades.

Softly she says,"It's as close as I can get to the forest. I shouldn't say such things – we haven't indentured anyone. Vilhan noticed you're not wearing the pendant, and mentioned it to my father."

"Norton and Vilhan... ...always..." He edits this thought, searches her. "How much have you forgotten?" he asks almost to himself, shocked.

"Leave my husband alone," she says darkly.

"If it weren't for-"

"We must not have this conversation again. I-" she seems to wrestle her temper down, sitting up straight again.

Fenur waits.

Using a diminutive in her own dialect, she asks,"How much have we forgotten, my little Fenur? How much do you remember? To remove the pendant is to leave yourself open. Once mine, always mine. Surely you remember that much." A strange caring act of possessiveness, Fenur struggles with. Her voice has gone down in volume. Leanor oddly arch against the statement, her back straight just how tall and lordly she is becomes apparent again to him. "Do not impugn the judgment of those above your station." Also in the old language, but seemingly empty from her.

"I remember what happened when those above my station failed. I also remember that I am my own soul, with or without your houses' pendant. I have my own power. And-"

"Not if you continue to remove your pendant," she interrupts him. "The others will not accept it. Do so at your own peril." A warning, not a command.

"I will do what I must."

"You SHOULD NOT INTERFERE," she stops, fists balled but regaining control, almost out of her chair,"You will not interfere by becoming part of the living stream of this world. That man, Scasey, who you saw on the way into my office has sensed us. He has alerted the gaming commissioner – even at your place as a dealer on the floor, certainly you know of them? The gaming commissioner has in turn alerted my superiors here at the casino. We must remain under cloak. We will find a way home. The horse on your" - she struggles to remember the word, translating some of the more foreign words takes her a moment, especially in her anger, her employees count it as aphasia - "...car; we had horses on our side. There must be a way back! There must be at least one naturally connecting passage. If you have acquired your trophies through any but natural means, the house of Nor will have their share. On this side or our own."

"I saw horses on television. Not just drawings or paintings like on the side of the car, but the real thing. And I had the same thought. That our two worlds must have connected many times."

"Careful boy or I will remind you of what you were." She stares him down.

A moment passes.

"And I will remind you," he says finally, quieter, rising for the door.

5.

"It's been in how many wars – in my family for how long? It's split granite. Why would some stupid gun put a nick in it?" Tartus wonders from behind the welding goggles, as the night wind blows through his hair in the open compartment.

"Maybe it was already there?" offers Tihan.

"Impossible. I polish it once a day, on schedule."

"You know, I think my favorite thing about this land we ever discovered was that nurbinium fools metal detectors," Tarnus says.

"Tartus, I apologize for impugning the family of Tar," Tihan says sheepishly.

"No, it seems... formal to me is all. Not informal. You are like family to me, Tihan, and I would not keep you at that kind of distance, and even though I know how you meant it..."

"Here, let's pull off here," says Tarnus. "Fenur's work?" asks Tihan. "This is not a defensible castle."

"Yeah..." "Don't you think we should be lying low?" asks Tartus.

"Who are they going to tell? What are they going to say if they do? That they saw a naked midget who made a fool of them and got away? And Love Jonze doesn't want trouble."

"They never remember us anyway, practically, unless we return often," offers Tarnus.

"Naked?" asks Tartus.

"Element of surprise. I had to get out of that alley somehow," says Tihan defensively.

"You flashed the LVPD?" Tartus asks.

She makes a gesture akin to a shrug.

Tarnus laughs heartily as he stomps on the brakes, which scream in protest. He bounds down, and digs in his coat as a valet walks up looking miserable about having to drive the old LRII A forgetful Tarnus pulls a one dollar bill out of a pocket and hands it to the valet.

"Sir, thank you, Sir." The valet's statement of gratitude dripping with irony, crushes the dollar bill into a pocket and frowns at them as he accepts the keys to LRII.

As the valet drives off, Tarnus asks,"What was that about?" The others dismiss it.

Lifting the welding glasses off his eyes again, Tartus says,
"Come on."

They tried to order at the bar and were turned away because of the late hour. The three wander from lobby to lobby and back outside, colorful turrets, a pastel castle, dissonant against caricatures of skyscrapers down the street. They sit at a bus stop bench, having found a mini-mart, and drink strong malted liquor out of a paper bag. They down several of the bottles, nursing them, police cruise by, slow... the cruisers look them over and leave.

Tartus says looking at the high walls,"It used to be you could ride into this town with a sack full of gold and exchange it for money; which is strange. Gold is money! But those days... This must have been a real land then. A real place for us."

"Still, we were lucky to arrive here when we did," Tarnus offers in return. "We couldn't have known that as we entered the lifestream of this world that the language of the land would come to us, or that we would find work that suited us. Or anything."

Pre-dawn makes the different architectures blend into something wholly new.

They are nearly asleep in an alcoholic doze when the first bus, a trial hydrogen vehicle stops in front of them. Shaking the damp from their coats, and stretching, they climb aboard. They take the bus to the airport where they wait for their transfer, the transfer in turn takes them into the desert. At a dusty sagebrush stand they disembark and wait.

"I feel like I did during the siege at Kragsteeth," says Tihan offhandedly trying to shake off sleep deprivation and the long night of excitement.

"Ah, now there was a dark day," Tarnus replies.

Tartus says,"It was a beautiful city. I will never be able to forgive myself for what I did."

"Tartus, you did what was necessary. What could you have done differently? The accumulation would have taken the city. Taken the libraries and ...our entire culture would have become but food to them."

"To burn such a wonder... how could I have?" he asks the desert more than his friends.

"You gave us a chance," Tihan says.

"Those ungrateful bastards. They'll never admit what you did. Never. They would have perished with us if you hadn't created the archway at the Pass of Heaven," Tarnus says. "They would rather have let all their slaves die. Would have rather dropped to the rocks below out of sheer egoism than thank you." Tarnus watches the bus approach out of the horizon line.

"But the diaspora..." Tartus starts.

"Or challenge the accumulation? Then?" Tihan asks him. "It would have been suicide."

"For those with no foresight. For those who make war for profit. And we do not fight." Tartus pulls the welding glasses down to settle over his eyes, as the daylight beckons.

The bus stops. "I hate the bus," Tarnus says.

The three climb aboard the work bus, flashing secure work area passes. On the bus sit other miners. "I hate not having my own tools to work with."

"I hate not sleeping," replies Tihan.

After the bus deposits the three at the entrance to the parking lot, two military personnel check their I.D. tags, and wave them through into the compound. A large parking lot falls away down a hillside flanking a railroad track and helicopter pads. A monorail tram, at the end of the parking lot up steep steps. A small tram station which was recently white but has faded to dun. Men in hardhats with clipboards walk into the railway lines. They check the numbers on railcars. Cranes move cargo off the railway lines and onto the local rails, while the tram transports people above. The tram lines descend into the mountain dig.

Earthmoving equipment deposits rubble around the mine – vastly oversized roads worm out of the valley. Three story high trucks move along these routes carrying the excavated rubble for depositing in designated areas.

A gated area and access road where workers' cars turn into the parking area There, the road continues on into the mountain next to the dual tramlines Giant digging machines sit in the sun, in front of warehouses of extra parts while mechanics work on them.

Multi-person electric carts swoop through the enormous parking lot picking people up at waystations.

"Maybe we can have a phosphor dump into the tunnels again. That was fun," says a man to someone he rideshares with as they settle in for the short trip down to the tram station.

"Harry, don't even make jokes like that," says Tartus gruffly, overhearing the two men.

"Sorry, sir," says the man, "Won't happen again."

"Trust me, I'm glad to see you're alert for every possibility," Tartus offers.

The man brightens.

The three shuffle up the steps in line to the top of the tram platform somewhere in the middle of the mass of morning workers. At the top the wait for the tram, staring at the safety warnings: HARDHAT ONLY, NO WIRELESS DEVICES, NO SMOKING, CHECK YOUR AREA. The push through the mass and collect hardhats out of stacks of shelving built into the tram platform. They pull rad cards from pockets and clip them to shirts.

The tram arrives, maglift electric, it makes a soft hissing as it approaches. The hydraulic doors are louder than the tram itself as they bang open when it stops.

"Finally back underground where we belong," Tihan says.

"You say that every morning. And every morning it grates on me worse than the time before," says Tarnus stepping aboard.

"Not at work," Tartus says softly.

Tarnus looks over at him, an affirmative gesture.

The tram doors close, and the three plant their feet and sway slightly while those who are taller hold on to rings in the ceiling of the tram. A gentle slope as the tram heads downward.

Below through the windows of the tram, on the road next to the railways system, earthmoving equipment rolls upwards through the half-light at this end of the dig, bringing dirt to the top side. The earthmoving machines screech and burble and thunder like underground monsters.

"How long have you been with us, Tartus?" asks the tall man in slacks and a denim shirt, a look Tartus perceives as the foreigner trying to fit in.

The office is small, inside the dig and out of the sun, opposite and higher up than Tartus' own. Still no one really pays attention to it, or the man from the outside world who is officially in charge of the site.

"My crew has been with you since you found the vein of gold," Tartus wraps his arms around his stocky torso and pivots back and forth on the balls of his feet.

"You have all been doing such a great job with the build; how do you think it will carry over into the everyday of maintenance?" asks the governmental overseer.

"I don't know. I'm not sure we thought we would stay on the dig this long. Once the vein was found... We bore easily, but I suspect we will stay on. At least for a while."

"Like you said, boredom sets in. Quality won't slip?" The man has his feet on his desk and his arms behind his head, as he insults Tartus' team.

Tartus reflects that in another life this would have been a blood offense. "No, Tom," he says quietly,"No, it won't." He hopes his tone will be mistaken for concern, rather than controlled rage.

"We still may need to downsize as the end of the dig. The end of construction approaches."

"Yes, I understand."

"Think about it. Think about who you really need." The official takes his feet off his desk, and goes back to reading files.

Back out in the construction, Tartus, unused to taking orders from anyone, pauses for a deep breath, and moves back towards his office.

Tihan's rad card checks low green in the deepest parts of the mine. Her office looks down on the tram unloading area. Her office midway up the side of the cavern, buried in a scaffolding structure which runs back along a cavern wall. She checks the rad card again. Over her the great wall, as they call it, turns, a leaded Teflon fiber, steel reinforced and blast resistant Plexiglas structure. (Amazing stuff Teflon. If only they could sell it back home.) The great wall turns from the center on a microns thick oil bearing. The disk shape allowing the cargo containers of rail cars, once they have been separated from the tram to be raised up inside the storage area via crane. The seal of the great wall closes behind so that the nuclear material can be offloaded without risk of contamination. Workers take the insides of the rail cars delivering cement-encased leaded containers of spent uranium rods, and bury the packets deep in the earth.

Raw uranium ore is also delivered for processing.

To one side, also behind the radiation seal, another large hallway descends in a different direction at an angle to the main dig. Down that way lies an unusual smelting plant separating the raw ore into its radioactive uranium and depleted uranium isotopes. The depleted uranium a less radioactive but still ultra dense metal the locals use for armor and weaponry. Sometimes military vehicles pass through the seal, disappearing down that way, requisitioning the material for use. Fissionable rods also emerge occasionally from that area for shipment to parts unknown to her.

The great wall, the twelve-story rotating disk, has a lone pie slice shaped hole, which closes and seals the underground dig site and storage area. It reminds her a little of home. On this side a specialized crane passes the railway shipping containers full of nuclear waste through the perforation in the wall to another specialized crane runing away into the burial area. The cranes on both sides have their own rail system running along the ceiling of the dig allowing them to move through the burial site interior or in the outside area along the tramway without affecting the flow of work below.

The wall's one pie slice hole acts as a safety device and can close on springs and hydraulics which hold a special door at bay against the inside of the disk. If any of the nuclear waste inside were to escape from the shipping containers, that amount of time it would take the slice shaped door to close would still be enough to kill every digger. But it would save the surrounding settlements. In times of low work or maintenance the slice out of the wall is rotated to the down position to allow machinery, the occasional military convoy headed to the smelting plant, and people through.

In other areas of the dig they have found silver (enough to make everyone of them fantastically wealthy back home), a little gold (pity) and uranium ore strikes. Plus traces of aluminum, rhodium, more...

Her card still reads green. She taps it, knowing it is useless.

Her mine training is focusing down. Something is wrong.

She picks up a wall phone and dials a code.

"Tartus here."

"Something – I don't know."

"I'm on my way," he says and hangs up. No argument like she would get from one of the taller ones. How long have they worked together? There's no need.

Minutes later he's standing with her, watching the operations at the wall. "You're right," he says. "Get Tarnus."

When he arrives he says,"My beard's prickling." "You said it," agrees Tihan.

"We've got to go in," Tarnus says.

Tartus picks up a phone. "We have a reading down here, we're coming in. No, I'm not ready to change the alert yet."

They walk over to the rail crane. The cranes attach to the gantry system hanging from the cavern walls on either side of the seal. The three climb up on to the track system for the cranes – sheets of grating and tools have taken over the elevators for reaching the upper levels of the gantries for periods of the day's shift, so they forgo a ride. The three begin the climb up the ladder. The operator on the exterior crane stops when he sees Tartus.

Half way up, Tarnus says,"It's not the height that bothers me. It's that I'm not afraid of heights that makes me afraid when I look down." The woven steel mesh of the catwalk floors allows them to see down between their feet all the way to the bottom. Small designated work areas and break areas with donuts, coffee, and chairs dangle out in empty space.

"I always think it's worse to stop," replies Tihan.

At the top of the cavern, next to the exterior side crane, on the catwalk, Tartus gives an arm circle gesture to the overhead track operator that brings the other gantry on the interior side of the great wall to its touching point with the one they are standing on. Hydraulics move the split gantry into place. The noise is deafening as the gantries nose up to each other, the sound reverberating through the cavern. The catwalks exactly matching up. The slight give of the metal creating a barely noticeable wave at the lip of the two catwalks where the interior and exterior meet up.

The three cross over, through the empty slice in the great seal in its up position, into the interior of the mine.

Below they board an electric car, and the driver asks,"Where to, Tartus?"

"Heart of the dig," says Tartus.

They travel down along an asphalt road, and out of the main construction into a darker area, lit only by arc lights spaced every fifty yards. The ceiling of the mine has come down to just over their heads. Talk of family from the driver as they journey through the dark. A fellow digger with children, grandchildren, even greatgrandchildren, some part of another clan the mix is so diverse and deep, he talks on as he drives, some felled by the accumulation, others lost without word, a few at the dig. "This is it: end of the line," says the driver. The road stops in front of them.

"I'm sorry we haven't spoken in so long, Tartus. It was good to catch up," Tartus says as the three hop off the car.

"Talked your beards off!" Tartus shouts back, and whirs away back towards the light.

"Torches?" says Tartus, taking out a full-sized Maglite.

The three walk, passing miners in orange jump suits, yellow hardhats, carrying drills with four foot corkscrew implements, or jackhammers. Another area, where the workers are on break, eating out of lunchboxes. Smell of canned soup still warm in thermoses, sweat, and cordite. They feel suddenly more at home.

"It's really bad now," Tarnus says. "My beards tingling so bad I almost want a shave."

"Blasphemy," says Tartus, meaning it as a joke, but it comes out as something much darker.

"They've figure it out haven't they?" asks Tihan.

Tartus presses into the hewn wall. "I can feel them deep inside."


6.


The card game in the penthouse winding down. In the distance, the sky has changed, still black but Fenur can tell it's nearly dawn. The stars here disorienting to him.

Stephen, the hotel's owner, folded an hour ago, never willing to truly lose any house money. He sits, in the meditative state of someone enjoying a good game.

Fenur stares out the window towards the Leanor's office. He wonders if she watches them through her telescope. Self-consciously he avoids looking in that direction. Norvil watching him.

Across from him, the Finn sits with his cards, chewing a cigar in a suit Fenur can tell he thinks is expensive.

"That's it, I fold," says the mid-western businessman. He shouldn't be here in this room. It's a sense of adventure they all get until they get home and they realize they can be followed to Tacoma or Iowa City or Bismarck. Fenur wonders what those places look like, and why they aren't immortalized here on the strip.

"Smart man, smart man." says the Finn.

Norvil wearing shades. He sits across the deep green table from where the chips are piled in front of the Finn. "What about you, little Fenur?" Norvil asks sharply.

"Nothing little about him. How tall are you, Fee?" asks the Finn an angry humor he senses is directed at Norvil. To the others:

"He must be seven feet tall. How do you two know each other anyway?" Detecting the tension between the two, he directs the question towards Norvil. Neither of them answers.

Filling the silence the Finn says,"He's almost tall enough he can see over my hand. But you can trust your dealer. Right, Fee?" Fenur senses a moment passing between Norvil and the Finn. The Finn looks at his chips, smiling at Norvil in the strange angry way of the locals.

It irks Fenur to be characterized this way by Norvil, but he's fairly sure it's just strategy on the part of this older member of the house of Nor.

"You gonna fold too?" the Finn asks Fenur. Fenur shakes his head no as is the custom.

Norvil guffaws and makes a clan specific affirmation, making a half-hearted attempt at replying while thinking about other things. He says,"Me either Fold? No, not yet." Which seems vacant at best.

"Let's take a break after this round," says Stephen.

Before the next round of cards Fenur goes into the bathroom to decompress. He uses the servant bathroom - the penthouse suite has everything including a slightly separated servants quarters. He guesses Stephen had the butler dismissed for the evening so they could play cards in peace. No stranger to being servile, he tries not to let it get to him.

By comparison to the other card players, other than Norvil of course, he hardly ever needs such amenities as toilets, water and the shower. Running water soothes him, but need is a different matter. Still, a moments refuge from Norvil gives him a little serenity. He sits on the ledge of the sink, listening to the still strange electric hum of the lights and waits while the others use the main facilities of the penthouse. Boyish jokes exchanged, new drinks poured.

Norvil in the doorway. "We're ready." Fenur stands.

"They were all using the other bathroom; I told them I would make do back here."

Fenur assents, unengaged.

"Fenur..."

"Yes, Norvil?"

"I saw you with a small vial of the oil. Do you still have it?" It's not really a question. Norvil still assuming he can bully Fenur into what he wants. A long habit of his, which he has not abandoned.

"I don't have it anymore." Norvil lunges at him and grabs him by the lapels of his tuxedo. "Yes, you do!" whisper-shouting, Norvil shakes him, and Fenur lets him, hanging on the inside seams of the expensive jacket. Norvil lowers his voice. "I need it. You have it. I command you to give it to me."

Fenur smiles. "You command nothing anymore. It is all for the better."

Norvil draws back his fist, and says,"She loved you no more than her true husband. DO you think because of one act you can assume command?"

"I desire to command no one."

"Not even yourself?" Norvil thinking better of it, lowers his fist, glancing out past the servant's quarters at the main room. So like before – making sure no one can see what he is doing. Like Vilhan. Instead, Norvil shoves Fenur back against the sink and storms out of the bathroom.

Fenur rechecks himself in the mirror and returns to the card table.

Technically, Fenur is still dealing. After so many rums or bourbons (a lot of bourbon; one of the tourists always says it's "old school" and he can never puzzle out exactly what they mean by this) or vodka rocks, they forget his hands. He can keep the depth of the deck in his head, knows the probabilities in the cards by the deepness of his cutting. From what he gets in his hand he can guess what went out, and what still lurks in the deck.

Norvil folds, discomfited against the table. His legs too long. He smiles, crumbling. "Take it." The Finn laughs at Norvil's misfortune.

"Well, I'm done for the evening gents," says the out-of-towner, picking up his coat, trying to rearrange a business shirt over a sizeable gut and wadding a tie into a pocket while straightening suspenders. "Have a nice morning."

"I'm gone too," says Stephen.

The Finn stubs out a cigar. "Yeah. That's it, gentlemen." He coughs from somewhere deep inside. "Fee, you need any work?"

"Work?" asks Fenur.

Norvil hides a half-smile behind a politely balled fist to his mouth, finding the subject distasteful and embarrassing when mentioned in public.

"Yeah, you know, you want do a few more of these, maybe help out at the factory level... You know what I mean?"

"No."

Stephen pretends not to hear as he gathers his coat, his chips, counts. Oblivious.

"The old man, he has plenty of projects. We got this new guy in town. Never met him. I know you better than I know him; maybe you could help us keep an eye on him."

"For money?"

"Yeah, for money. We wouldn't expect you to do it for free," the Finn seems to find this almost funny.

"Maybe," Fenur says, not sure the Finn is serious.

"Ok, look - when's the next time you're on the floor? Tomorrow night? I'm going downstairs to grab an hour or two of sleep." Meaning a cheaper room, though he would never say those words directly. "I'm meeting the old man out at the Las Vegas Speedway at noon. You want the work; be there."

Fenur nods in the way of locals.

After they've gone, Norvil says,"Fenur, it's unwise to play with the slipstream like this."

Fenur says nothing. Then reconsiders,"Instead I should give you my remaining oil so you can?" Looks out the panoramic window of the penthouse. The place seems suddenly lonely. On the wall hang the locals' masterpieces. Rembrandts and Hockneys side by side in Stephen's warped world. Fenur thinking about how much he would like to be out of the penthouse suite.

"If only..."

Fenur looks up at him, eyes hooded in the poorly illuminated hotel room. "If only so many things, Norvil."

Norvil changes tack, saying,"Leanor says you have been removing your pendant of life while you work."

"She said one of her watchers had seen."

"So it is true?" Norvil asks. Fenur senses a hint of anger somewhere behind the question.

"If I were to forsake the heritage of the houses, it would be mine alone to forgo – my people never believed the pendants helped. I owe the house of Nor nothing. And my own house, were it here to complain, would not want me now. You have taken enough from me. Let me be on this." Fenur starts to grab the chips off the table, putting the bigger denominations in his breast pocket, the medium ones in either side pocket by color. The smaller ones he puts in pants pockets; stops, fishes a medium size chip out. "Here, Norvil, tell her I gave this to you, so you don't have to return to her empty handed."

Fenur turns to leave.

"You are only free because of your valor at the Pass of Heaven. But you were valorous because of the clay people. The short ones would not give you the credit you are due. You cannot join one of their clans. Where would you go if not to us and our customs?"

"Never to my own kind as represented in the houses," Fenur says over his shoulder as he walks to the private elevator door.

"Once a slave, always a slave. Who will you turn to when the time to go home comes? Who will protect you from the accumulation?"

"We will not be going home. This is what you miss in chastising me about the pendant. Who will protect me, should it come to it? I will. As I did before. As I protected you with the help of the clay people," he spits the words, hating how derogatory they sound. "You who would have rather died, brought us all low, made us one with the accumulation. What kind of leaders were you that I should despair of losing my heritage to this place?" The elevator arrives and Fenur boards. Before the door closes he says,"Let me remind you, if I had not removed my pendant then, we all would have perished."

7.

"Hey, it's Fee. Our ace in the hole. How's it going?"

Fenur walks along the rows of metal seats toward a group of middle-aged men. A man who might be Asian sits behind their row.

"I'm well," says Fenur taking a seat.

The Las Vegas Speedway is hot going on boiling even at a little after noon. Every time the wind blows the metal rows of seats give off furnace-like heat. Below them along the circuit is a practice racing session. Formula motorcycles scream around the circuit, flattening out tachometers at eighteen thousand plus rpm, speeds on straightaways upwards of two hundred miles per hour. The riders slam from corner to corner, g-forces trying to pull heads and helmets from riders' bodies. At the west end of the track a hairpin where the bikes lean over far enough to drag knees and knuckles. The more complex track ringed by an old-fashioned circular speedway. A hive city of trucks, camper vans, medical tents and makeshift tool and die shops has sprung up next to the exhibition.

The man in the middle, the Finn from the previous night card game, slightly overweight, looks at the older man next to him and says," This is the kid I was telling you about."

"What?" asks the older man. Even in the heat he's wearing a sport jacket. Fenur tries to place the make, but finally decides it's handmade to order.

"The one with the red car the Enzo's kid made; you remember."

"You got that old red mid-engine I see driving all over town?" asks the older man.

"Yes," says Fenur.

"You like motorcycle racing?" "I don't know anything about it," Fenur confesses.

"Ah..." spits the old man," Your accent. Seems like Europeans like it. You aren't from Europe?"

"No," Fenur says.

"It's useless: no one bets on it." The old man seems affable enough about it. "My son's a tech for the Repsol team. Abandoned Bologna for the Japs – can you believe it?" The old man is almost shouting. "Anyway, I came to watch him work."

"You know what this kid has done for the vig, with the double downs on Sunday night?" says the overweight man.

The old man looks at the Finn, then over at Fenur. Quiet.

Finally," Never cared for the stabled horses," says the older man to Fenur," That company he drove for – the fascistas. There was a car." "They're all gone," says Fenur.

"Yeah, Russian steel. They all rusted away. It's the way all things beautiful go," the older man turns back to the practice. "Never lasts."

"True enough," says Fenur into the wind, translating a much older phrase into English.

The old man satisfied with Fenur's response changes subjects. "The Finn here, he says you got something special. Some sort of jinx on the cards."

"I can feel them better than most people," Fenur offers. The Finn says,"All the card counters, we put them in a room with Fee, but his luck turns them, no matter how deep they can count. They're always a little off. Fee's some sort of statistical anomaly."

"You betting against yourself or your casino? You must not be hurting for work you're driving that deathtrap," says the old man.

"I'm good at what I do. I play a few rounds in my off hours."

"A few rounds? Finn says you must be pulling down a couple of million a year. You take work from anybody else? We can't be having a conflict of interest," the old man still watches the motorcycles turning through the course.

"I play for myself when the mood suits. I sit in a round where I deal, when they let me." "You must be pretty good," the old man offers, bating him.

"I am," Fenur says simply.

"'Cause Finn thought maybe you worked for that queeny type over there that manages the spurting fountain of pomp and circumstance. The fancy place down there at the end of the strip. That maybe you're playing her against the manager over at your hotel - looks like you could be related. We couldn't figure out how though. Maybe you got something going with him?"

"Not anymore. When I was young I had a debt with Leanor I had to work off," says Fenur truthfully.

"That why you don't work or live over there?" "That's right," says Fenur.

The old man, not letting go of it asks,"You two aren't family; you and that...?" the old man looks at the Finn, waiting for him to fill in the name.

"Norvil."

"Yeah, Norvil at the hotel," the old man looks to the Finn, who writes something down, nodding. "Where's your family from?"

"We aren't related. My family's from the East. Norvil's from the Mountains. We're both tall. That's it, as far as similarities."

The old man puts a pair of binoculars to his eyes and watches the pit. The Japanese team running a dyno on an identical bike. "That kid..."

"Smart little bastard you got there, Lou."

"Tell me about it." Without taking the binoculars down he says,

"Finn..." The overweight man nods.

"You see this guy behind us?" asks the Finn.

Fenur looks back, even though he remembers what the man looks like. He does it because the locals are more at ease with actions that suit their own social order. He does it because the man behind him exudes a menacing aloofness that makes Fenur uncomfortable. This uncommon feeling has made him work hard to ignore the man behind him. "We want to find out if he's the real deal or more some sort of Hideki Irabu."

Fenur stares at him. "Ok, you don't follow. You from back east; you sure?"

"Very sure."

"Don't follow baseball, I guess. Back east, they pay this guy a fortune. Big hitter in Japan. He gets to the Yanks and it doesn't happen for him."

"Hideki Irabu?" asks Fenur.

"Yeah," confirms the Finn.

"Anyway, what are you going to do with an American League team? They don't even let their pitchers – Ho!" exclaims the old man. One of the motorcycles goes down, the rider low-siding out into gravel, legs extend at one point and body rolling, cartwheeling, trying to scrub off speed. The bike ruptures sending parts and shrapnel flying.

"That's one of Freddie's guys, I think," the Finn says.

The old man looks at the Finn. "Amateurs, racers – when's that lunatic going to field a real team?"

"He did."

"Ah-" the old man makes some cryptic hand signal at the Finn and goes back to looking through the binoculars.

"I came to see you about-" Fenur starts, trying to lead the conversation back his way.

The bike rider stands up, swaying, runs to check the bike.

Kicks it and storms away.

The old man continues as though he hasn't heard Fenur.

Scratches a few days worth of old man's white beard as he talks.

"This guy behind us? He's on loan to us from the yaks out of Yokohama. No? Yakuza? Ok. Anyway, these guys are helping us out around the Pacific Rim – Macau's the new big thing - a couple of hiend casinos going in, where we're partnered up. The Macanese, they can't use their own – the State would come down on them cracking heads. Ocean. Sunsets. Yachts. Monetary exchange or Forex-"

"Lou..." the Finn cautions.

"...Etcetera, etcetera." The old man stops himself, says to the Finn, but pointedly for Fenur,"What? Who's the kid gonna tell?" He watches the track for a moment. "Other than desert vultures."

The Finn looks back at the Japanese man. A definite edge to him, despite his small stature. "We need a favor; you do us the favor..." the Finn shrugs,"...whatever you want."

"The Finn says he trusts you, you run an honest game. We can use an inside man. Especially a floater like yourself. You deal the game honest to the Finn as long as he can remember. You're lucky. He remembers that too. We like lucky. Stephen... That crazy suit..." laughs the old man. "He doesn't have enough problems with that Norvil stealing from him; pretty soon we're going to have all his Rembrandts!" the old man, whose name is actually Luigi Vertosi, laughs. The laugh ends in a hacking cough. "Sato!" shouts the old man. The man in the Japanese designer suit looks up. "It's time."

"Hai!" says the Japanese man.

"Go with Fee." Fenur gets up, and Sato stands as well.

"You were going to ask something earlier? What was it you wanted anyway?" asks the Finn.

Fenur shrugs it off, shakes his head like a local to indicate everything has been answered to his satisfaction.

"Ok," says the Finn, grabbing Fenur's taller shoulder and walking him away. When Sato, Fenur and the Finn are off the bleachers, the Finn hands him an envelope. "For a good game, and for driving our friend around. Stay out of the that rattletrap red cockmobile, Ok?" The Finn laughs.

"I got it," says Fenur.

Fenur drives, not looking at Sato in the passenger seat. Sato, for his part, manages to ignore Fenur. Fenur has never worked for Vertosi before, but it's clear what they're after. He heads towards a car rental office south of the airport, parking in short term parking.

"My people - the Far Sea people used what they called - call," he tries to correct himself,"-windrunners, which was a type of hot air balloon, and tethered kites for as long as they could remember, traveling from island to island. Using smaller versions as message relays. Sailing in the water, sailing through the air." Fenur long ago learned that locals will hardly ever remember him, unless he makes a point of it. He has taken to saying what he wants, and relying on their faulty memories. For the first time he worries that maybe he will be remembered.

Sato says nothing. They wait for a bus from airport parking in the glaring heat.

"I didn't know why, but someone told me recently why he is called the Finn while I was dealing out a game."

Sato turns and looks at him briefly, goes back to looking down the isles of traffic coming into the airport. Fenur judges that maybe Sato understands what he is saying. Sato's eyes hunt for the next bus in the distance.

"It's because he swims through Vegas like a shark, but you never see more than the top of him. He's got a million deals going on, but you only see one piece of it." Sato ignores him. Fenur though worried about being remembered, is not exactly worried about his association with the mobsters, or this yakuza.

"You look like somebody to me," says Fenur, unsure of who it is. Sato looks over at him. Through him. Fenur's pendant of life suddenly throbs against his chest. It's a plaintiff vibration through him. It subsides.

Sato looks around the airport entrance and exit circuit.

"The bus is still ten minutes away," Fenur tries.

Sato rolls his shoulders and plants his feet.

After renting a gray sedan, paying cash and offering a dummy back-up credit card that came out of the envelope from the Finn, they are back on the road and headed for the strip. Along with the card, and a large roll of hundreds, Fenur found several numbered pieces of paper. On the next piece of paper in the series of directions is printed: 1. Hotel on strip, room 608. 2. Return to Fremont St. Garage. A large blue sedan.

A car key in the envelope as well. The first two notes dealt with the airport pick-up of the first car and bus times.

"You sure this is right?" asks Fenur. Fenur holds the paper up for Sato.

"Hai," mutters Sato, looking out the window, barely looking at the paper.

Fenur rolls into a parking garage, absent-mindedly grabbing a ticket - not that they will be returning to the car.

When they stop, Sato rubs down the car in a business-like fashion trying not to be noticeable about it, but not missing anything either. Satisfied, he slings a bag across a shoulder. One sharp nod.

Fenur follows him down a flight of stairs, and they walk along the strip.

Fenur splits off from Sato, headed toward the car that has been rented for them.

Later he's cruising back down the strip. Cruises through the loading area wearing a pair of dark sunglasses, knowing the big sedan doesn't stick out. It has plates from somewhere called the Mid-West, another characteristic Fenur understands makes it completely immune to visibility. Sato raises a hand in the loading zone, foot traffic and shuttle vans swirling around him, out of his way, current eddies against a stone. Fenur stops the car, leans over and pops the door for him.

Sato slides down into the seat hands on his bag in a practiced way so that he isn't touching the interior of the car. "Yoroshii," he nods.

8.

The tedious ride back from the dig, an hour into the desert every day, and an hour back to the city. The commute, in the summers especially, is brutal.

"You sometimes call me Ti," Tihan says returning to the conversation from the night before.

"It's a familiar form for... for – you know," Tartus says.

Tihan give him a questioning look.

"For females. You just had to hear me say it, didn't you?" Tartus pining.

"I think I've made my point."

"That we're all females?"

"That would make life simpler. Anyway, you know that's not how I think of myself."

"Would it? Where did we park?" asks Tarnus, ignoring this interchange, as the bus turns onto the strip.

"I don't know," Tihan says. "I'm still hung over."

"It's at the Joyeuse," Tartus says from behind the welding glasses, pulled down against the ferocious daylight stabbing through the bus.

"Those look ridiculous," Tihan offers as the bus rocks back and forth.

"The mine is the right brightness. The desert sun is not." Tartus offers no apologies.

The bus maundering through the disgorgement areas of the hotels along the strip, finally dropping them at the Joyeuse.

The pavement hot even through dirty boots after the day's long sun.

Tartus searching for a valet to fetch the LRII – finally disappearing into the air conditioning of the lobby to locate one.

"Shall we bury ourselves in our people's other great love besides digging?" Tihan asks.

"Gambling? I am short enough," Tarnus dejected.

"You're always short."

"You're right; but we should try and stay below ground and hope the locals forget."

"As they always do," she turns, still looking for a valet, pointing out,"You are afraid to gamble because you are unlucky."

"They cheat here," Tarnus replies.

Joking with each other to keep spirits up, as it has always been here, wasting time, waiting to fade from memory.

Suddenly a police car swoops to the side of the curb in the hotel entry and disembarking area.

A uniform saying,"Excuse me, sir," as another gets out of the passenger side door, hand on holster.

Tarnus and Tihan keep walking. Tartus has still not returned from the hotel's interior.

The uniformed police following Tarnus and Tihan. In a louder voice one of the uniforms says,"Please stop where you are!" He's holding a fax, and has a walkie-talkie raised to his lips.

The two headed away from the disembarking point for the hotel, out towards the strip, looking for Tartus, whom they hope has found the LRII.

Another police car pulling up into the passenger off-loading zone. The car makes a loud BLIP-BLIP noise as it pulls to the curb, blocking Tarnus and Tihan in. People scramble out of the way of the disturbance stopping further off to gawk. Tires squealing to a stop. Police out of the second squad car, hands on pistols as they crabwalk towards the two shorter figures.

"Stop!" shouts the another uniform. Even the hotel security hanging back.

Tartus nowhere to be seen.

"You heard the man," says another one of the cops.

Tarnus risks a glance over his shoulder.

"Yes, you two. I'm not going to ask again."

Finally, they see Tartus still on the inside of the hotel doors watching. They exchange a look with each other.

Tarnus and Tihan break into a run, but the cops expecting it, sprint after them. Tackled. Knees in backs while they are handcuffed. "We asked you to stop nicely." They are hauled up by handcuffs. Tihan throws out a boot and kicks the police car, leaving a muddy dent. "Yeah?" the cop asks Tihan. "You aren't going anywhere, my friend."

The tiny vintage automobile sits behind the police car, waiting.

Tarnus spots Fenur through the windshield. "Tihan?"

Tihan continues struggling as the police open the back door of the cruiser and try and force her in, her legs against the doorframe.

From the other side of the car Tarnus says,"Tihan! Look."

Tihan's head comes up, follows the jerk of Tarnus's head. She makes eye contact with Fenur. He's laughing. It's the last thing she sees as the cruiser door closes on her.

"Yeah – wow: it's red and ostentatious. Who would have thought you would have seen that in Vegas?" the other cop says to Tarnus, completely missing the point.

Tarnus in the other side forced down and clamped into the uncomfortable molded plastic seat.

"Yes. Hilarious," Tarnus says through the back window to Fenur.

Tarnus gives Fenur a rude gesture from the home.

The cops up front, closing doors with a solid thunk, and the cop on the passenger side rolls down the passenger window while gesturing to the security guard. The security guard hands the fax to the cops through the window. The one in the passenger seat pulls a clipboard off the front dash and begins writing.

"Where's the third one of you?" "What's that supposed to mean?" retorts Tihan.

"We don't know what you're talking about," Tarnus snarls.

"You were the three from the other night at the strip club down the way?"

"Love Jonze?" says the driver.

"Don't know what you're talking about," says Tarnus gruffly.

The cop in the passenger seat holds up the fax with his left hand, while continuing to write with his right hand. Security camera shots from the club. All three of them.

"Where's your partner?"

"You think just because we're all short and have beards we all look alike? Is that what it is?" shouts Tihan at them.

The cop writing the report rolls his eyes. Tarnus turns as far around as his cuffs will allow and looks at Fenur, drumming his hands on the steering wheel. Fenur gives a brief flicking finger wave as he continues to drum, waiting for the police car to pull out. Tarnus glares back at him. Tihan doesn't engage, but just watches the interaction.

Tarnus sees Tartus behind the door glass disappear back into the hotel, looking around, heading off for a different exit. As the police car pulls away, the two watch the red car find a hole in traffic; Fenur makes his way through the loading zone and back out into strip afternoon traffic. Makes a right, circling the hotel.

The police car continues on with the two of them.


9.



On the opposite side of the hotel Tartus is walking away. The vintage sports car slows next to the short figure in the glaring sun.

Fenur reaches over and rolls down the window on the passenger side "Hello, short one. Fancy a ride?"

Tartus looks over and into the window. Almost continues walking. Decide against it and pulls the car door open.

Inside the cabin smells musty, strange in that way that the tall ones are different, it smells of leather and distantly also of gasoline, oil; the comforting smells of mine shafts.

"Having a bit of trouble?" mocks Fenur.

"No," Tartus says curtly, taking it from the taller one, as the mid-engined V6 purrs in the hundred-plus heat.

"Because it looked like-" "There's no trouble. The locals will forget after tonight. I'll go later and bail the two of them out. It's nothing that hasn't happened before."

"The way you live, I'm not surprised."

"We still do something remotely related to our heritage," says Tartus.

"I live in a tall tower and surround myself with expensive things..." Fenur punches the gas for show and the V6 rattles its cage.

"And it has nothing to do with your heritage. Your heritage was the ocean, and the sky, which the house of Nor happily took from you," this is as gruff as Tartus can ever make himself with Fenur, as much as the boy could use a talking to. "What were you doing at the hotel? You aren't working today. I take it you saw the end of that encounter?"

"Parking is full all along the strip – my work has more from being more touristy. I was picking up a few things from work and going to get a shave and haircut when I saw the... altercation."

"I see," says Tartus noncommittally.

"So if everything's going so well, where's the LRII?" smirks Fenur.

"I... decided to wait." He adds,"It's in the hotel's lot. I'll get it when things calm down.

Our contingency plan is one of us always gets away." Tartus realizing how feeble it actually sounds.

"Sounds familiar," Fenur intimates.

Tartus frowns. "It wasn't us short ones. You think I'm unaware?" Fenur says nothing.

A moment's awkward silence.

Fenur finally tries:"Remember that time you three stole all that sushi because you wanted to go on a blindfish binge, and it was the closest thing you could find?" Fenur laughs, trying to find a way through the uncomfortable thing between them.

After a minute or two, a stoplight, Tartus says,"What has become of us? Once we were..." he leaves it unfinished.

"You were. I was nothing. Worse than nothing. Want to see something?" Tartus looks over at him.

"I've got something you have to see. I will take you back over to the police station to bail them out later. The locals' memory of our stream will have faded, then you can pick up the LRII."

Tartus consents.

One of the hotel's staff brought up the crate of dark mead, which sits in the foyer of the penthouse suite. As the two step off the elevator, Tartus nearly trips over it.

He stares down at it as the elevator door closes. A fountain or a hot tub, Tartus can't decide, gurgles water, spilling over a side of marble to be recaptured. Wisps of steam fill the air over it. Even here the boy has found a way to be close to the sounds of the shore.

"I thought at first Leanor had sent it over." "Why?" asks Tartus, flummoxed. "Where...?" He tries again.

"Who?" Fenur shakes this off, not knowing.

Fenur picks the crate up and carries it gently to a coffee table in the main room. Vinyl records and a turntable on the floor in one corner, a small tube amp and large strangely flat speakers taller even than Fenur. An armoire stands with a door ajar and clothes falling out. More expensive clothes lie on the floor wadded in a heap.

"You're listening to their music now?" asks Tartus examining the music machine.

"I'm going native. I saw the gadgets at the electronics show last year. There's a store in town." Tartus sits down on the edge of a chair, his toes barely touching the floor. He stares at the crate.

"Hand me one of those. Those fools will be sorry they got arrested when I tell them." He lifts the welding goggles off his eyes to examine the mead.

"Be my guest," says Fenur, and hands Tartus one of the small bottles. He doesn't offer to find Tartus an instrument to open it. His own kind are unable to open the bottles, and Tartus' people do not need one.

Tartus grabs the top and grips it, breaking the seal placed on the mead. "Was always more of an ale man myself."

"I never enjoyed ale. And you know how we feel about the dark mead. The house of Nor was cruel enough without adding drink," says Fenur settling back into a couch and putting his feet up on the coffee table next to the crate, pondering it.

"Leanor delivered this?" The short one still boggling.

"She claims not."

Tartus grunts. "I didn't mean to imply personally."

Fenur laughs. Tartus has noted the boy's penchant for brooding before, and can hardly ever remember seeing him laugh. "Can you imagine?" asks Fenur.

"No," says Tartus, laughing gruffly.

"I have a bottle of the oil left," says Fenur suddenly. He seems surprised by this statement.

"How...?"

"How was this crate obtained?" Fenur ignores it haughtily, something the tall ones are known for, dismissing both questions. Tartus tries not to internalize this. It's part of who they are.

Tartus waits. From previous experience Tartus knows eventually Fenur will speak up if given time. He drinks the dark mead and waits.

"One of the slaves passed it to me through the bars at Wind's Breath. They stole it from the house." Meaning the oil, not the mead.

"A fortune. This is why..." Tartus stops himself from wandering into an open discussion of the house of Nor.

"Go on," says Fenur stretching his arms behind his head.

"You aren't working tonight?" asks Tartus.

Fenur offering some small body language, nonchalant, uncaring. He explains, "I made money at a private game last night. There is another game tonight as I said. The hotel lets me set my own schedule, more or less. Finish your thought."

Tartus starts again, but with a more politic tone, "To misplace such a thing. To have so much, that a missing vial would go unnoticed. Perhaps we deserved-"

Fenur leaps forward and slams his fist on the crate where his legs were resting. The bottles jump. So does Tartus. "DESERVED? DESERVED THAT?"

Tartus lets him have the moment, remembering what the boy was forced to do. "I did not mean that what was required of you was in any way your fault. But you cannot escape your destiny. It is who you are, to have done what you did. We all would have perished if not for your actions. The house of Nor says what? You have no soul? So be it. To have a soul and for it to be the soul they claim to have... better to die and meet with oblivion. To become one with the stream again... it only means something if you have found absolution in your destiny." Tartus stops. Fenur is looking out the window.

Fenur rubs his eyes. "It is done. There is no more."

Tartus ponders the bottle of mead. "Do they know you have the oil?"

"No."

"Fenur, what you did for the underpeople will be remembered as long as we build and walk and dig. You will always be welcome among us. You became our kin that day. Why do you defend those who took so much from you?"

Fenur stares at Tartus, having nothing to say.

"Don't go down their path," Tartus offers. He sips the mead.

"What few crates were brought through... To find such a thing here."

"Take two for the others," Fenur asks him. "Send someone for the rest."

Tartus approving, scratches his beard and reaches down to pick two more of the dark mead bottles from the crate and stuff them in his digger's rucksack when the phone rings.

Fenur reaches for the hotel landline. Holds it to his ear.

Listens. "What?" He looks at Tartus.

Tartus raises his eyebrows, pushing the dark mead into the sack.

"A message from Leanor," Fenur says to Tartus. "Have any interest in seeing her?"

Tartus laughs.

10.

The two stand at Leanor's desk. Tartus drinking the remaining dark mead from the bottle he opened in Fenur's penthouse. Leanor watches this from behind steepled fingers while Tartus chokes back another laugh.

"Our last meeting was short. Since I have been informed Norvil is missing. Have you seen him?" Leanor addresses Fenur, ignoring Tartus.

"No," Fenur says. Tartus increasingly more agitated next to him.

"I see," she says, refusing to look at Tartus. Angry, nearly embedded in the deep burnished wood of the office. She drips with silver, Tartus calculates what it would be worth back home. Astronomical.

"Why are you asking the boy? Norvil's money troubles with the locals... a member of the houses could have easily taken matters into their own hands to obfuscate our presence. Just as easily we could be asking you what you did you do with Norvil." Tartus understanding how uneasy this will make Leanor, but saying it anyway – partly from being goaded by being ignored, partly because it is true and must be said.

Tartus can tell his words grate on her. He stops himself from prodding her again and rousing her ire. Still ignoring Tartus, she repeats,"My brother is missing. This is not some prank on the locals by a member of the houses." She turns and glares at Tartus. Then to Fenur,"If not out of fealty, will you help me out of shared destiny?"

Tartus looks at Fenur, having expected this. Notes Leanor's choice of words and his conversation with the boy back in his hotel room. Something in him rises up. He holds out the empty bottle of dark mead by the small part of the neck. A small amount of the almost sticky substance clings to the inside of the bottle. "Right here," he says, indicating his presence in the room. Two fingers hold the bottle.

"Why did you bring the clay?" Leanor asks Fenur.

Fenur says to Tartus sarcastically,"I'm sure she doesn't mean anything by it."

Tartus whirls and throws the bottle at the far wall where it explodes, a fountain of glass followed by a small fire ball; the blast hitting them with more heat and glare than should have been in such a small container. A moment later, the charred wall is all that remains.

Leanor jumps to her feet. "Are you mad!" she shouts.

"Perhaps," says Tartus. "But I will ask again, never the less; though I expect nothing of a tree such as yourself. Did one of you do something with Norvil?"

"You are here on sufferance and the treaty, which I choose to honor at this moment, but do not think that we could not crush you if we chose. How dare you blaspheme in such a way-"

"She treats everyone likes this, doesn't she?" asks Tartus. "And I thought only you had 'gone native.'"

"I just like the music."

"And the cars."

Fenur agrees. "And the cars."

Leanor sits again, heavily, watching them. "We didn't do anything with him. We have splintered as you know. After our argument at the Pass of Heaven we have barely spoken. Fenur is the only one who passes between the two camps. I have been trying to call a gathering."

"It's a good thing; his making his own decisions that day," Tartus offers.

Leanor stares across the desk at Tartus, now resettled in her throne-like chair, nearly burning holes in him with her eyes.

"I say his actions, and his... what do the local diggers say when they solve a problem at the site?" He looks down, trying to come up with the phrase,"'Thinking outside the box?' There would have been no arguing after. The leaders froze. No wonder he does not choose a side," Tartus adjusts, rolling his shoulders inside the dirty coat, feeling the chipped axe against his side. "If you had not warred upon the house of Nur and destroyed it, how would a boy cousin have been able to save you at the pass?"

"Tartus, it's alright..." whispers Fenur.

"You are a hero, boy, and they treat you as though you are still their slave," Tartus says quietly, placing a gentle hand up on Fenur's bicep. Leanor's rage at the affront turning to a kind of dull pain. Tartus turns to Leanor,"I have held my tongue until now, as you are not my family. He was the one who began the forging of the treaty. He was the one who entreated your factions to sign. And you had already seen what had happened to our clans. What had happened to his people at the Far Seas, while you slaughtered them. I'll ask you again: have you done something to Norvil?"

Leanor sighs. "The hotel is in serious debt. More so than the human Stephen the owner, knows. Norvil owes money to a friend of the Finn, who believe Fenur knows," she ends bitterly.

"I understand," says Tartus.

"What we have heard is that the Finn and his people were hiring an outside to resolve the issue," she puts her long elegant hands flat on the desk.

"Fenur, I'm asking you as Norvil's sister, what do you know of this? You know the Finn. What kind of person is he? Would he understand enough to hurt my brother?" she is nearly pleading.

Fenur stares down at her from across the desk. "Yes. He would.

What are you asking of me?" Tartus scratches his beard.

"You know them over there. You know the types that frequent the private games. Talk to them. As a favor to the house of Nor, which we have no right to ask of you..." she runs her hands down her dark green skirt, straightening it. She pushes palms flat against the desk and looks up at Fenur. "Once you loved me. Will you not help what is left our race?"

Tartus shifts, uncomfortable with the display of emotion.

"I loved you as a dog loves its master. My time as your pet ended at the pass above Wind's Breath. You would not choose, so I had to. If you had loved me, you would not have made me make the choice. It was a queen's responsibility. I will ask those I know of Norvil's disappearance. For his sake, and the sake of those who serve him," the last Fenur bites off.

"We will help." Tartus says gruffly.

Leanor's attention shifts to him.

"We will help look for your brother. We are nearly bound by the treaty of Kragsteeth to do so."

"Shall I pay you in dark mead?" she asks, attempting humor and failing.

"Did you send it?" Tartus asks directly.

"No. I am investigating who might have."

Downstairs, Fenur and Tartus find the monorail, and board, riding back to the pyramid.

"Norvil may be dead," says Fenur looking out at the city from aboard the monorail.

"I know," says Tartus.

"I may know what happened to him."

Tartus risks a look sideways at him as they wait amongst the locals for the monorail to arrive at its stop. He decides not to press.

11.

"Do you know they tried to de-louse us?" says Tarnus as he and Tihan exit the bulletproof glass door from the interior holding cells of the jail.

"Sorry we missed night court," Tartus greets them.

"They threw me in with him. With the males. Can you believe it?" Tihan asks.

Tartus opens his mouth to respond and is grateful to be interrupted by Tarnus saying,"What is he doing here?"

Fenur hunches, grabbing either elbow with an opposite hand. "You know he was laughing at us when we were taken away?" "Hard to believe," Tartus equivocates.

"How was night court?" asks Fenur.

"The locals..." Tarnus stops, realizing Fenur is having a joke on him. Tarnus turns red.

"Before you start shouting," says Tartus,"May I remind you this is a public place in a foreign land? And also: he put up the bail."

"Let's go," Tihan interjects before the situation turns sour.

They wait in a malformed line at a bulletproof glass window with a rotating pass-through. "Can't give you your tools back. Sorry," says a clerk behind the glass. The rest of their stuff comes back in an organized pile. Coats and laces for boots. A little money and their wallets. "Couldn't find your I.D.'s"

"Axes," says Tarnus. "We need the axes. They're our livelihood."

"Sorry. If the charges are dropped or you're found innocent you can come by and collect them from evidence when the proceedings are over."

"That was my father's axe," says Tarnus, nearly pleading.

Fenur's smile is drying up.

Tartus places a gentle hand on Tarnus's shoulder. "Come on. It's only a month or so. The axe is older than all of us together. It will last that long in here."

Tartus looks around. Tarnus finds Tihan's eyes, and Tihan confirms. "We'll get them back, Tarnus," says Tihan. They pull on him gently until he turns away.

"It's a good thing you are all small," says Fenur. The three find a way to fit into the passenger seat and on to the floorpan, one over the engine cover in the cramped space behind the two seats.

"Very funny," says Tihan, getting the passenger side floor.

"Relax," says Fenur,"You'll be back in that big scary green contraption before you know it. It's a five minute ride back to the strip."

In the parking lot they find the LRII. Tartus has related the meeting with Leanor to the other two squashed into the seat with him on the short drive back.

"Fenur..." Tartus says. He stops. Fenur looks at him expectantly, ready to be gone about his business. "I meant what I said. We will help you look for Norvil. But there's something else you should know."

"Yes?" "Are we really going to tell them," huffs Tarnus. "We have no choice," says Tartus. He turns back to Fenur,"I don't know everything that has happened to you. Or how you think you are involved in what may have happened to Norvil. But..."

Getting out of the car first, followed by the others, Tihan says,"We think the accumulation may be about to break through at the dig."

"What?" Fenur asks, the expanse of parking lot and surrounding city seeming to small to hold his surprise. "Break through? The energy of the dig site you said masked the transfer point up in the old silver mines to the north. You said the mages-"

"The mages of stone picked it as carefully as they could, but it was still a wild throw of the axe. The accumulation has its own devices. We must see the last mage, and bring him to the site of transference in the old silver mines. See if the point where the boundary is weakest has really been drawn to the dig as we thought it might be."

"We will perish. Even the locals..." Fenur says shocked.

"They will meet the same end as us. And they are unprepared for the opening and transfer. They have no basis with which to deal with it."

"We can not - YOU PROMISED ME-" he shouts.

"Those that died would have died with or without promises," says Tartus. "But I swear this to you, Fenur. I will not allow this to happen to these people while my blood still flows and I can grasp a haft."

"I am lost," Fenur says simply and turns on them, doubling over, and choking back something terrible. In a moment he recovers, breathing deeply. They hear a bitter laugh as he closes the door on the red car and starts the engine. Fenur drives away.

"All things considered, I think he took it rather well," says Tarnus.

"Something has happened to him. He is changed. I worry for him," says Tartus.

"He knows something he's not saying," replies Tihan, a note in her voice the other two have trouble placing.

"He said he thinks he may be responsible for Norvil disappearing."

"Bah!" spits Tarnus, grasping the driver's side door of the LRII. "Children always think they are responsible for adults' mistakes."


12.


Light creeps in through windows, sun blocked out by exposed film glued directly to the windows, or tattered blinds and shutters with broken mattes. The interior is slightly too warm. It's dusty, but not dirty or grimy. Detritus of the surrounding civilization piles on counters or under them, vintage and tossed-off clothing hung haphazardly on rusting racks, where the occasional moth can be seen fluttering away from a moldering line of jackets. The clothing similar to what the three are wearing.

In a corner metal scraping sounds as they close the door behind them, blocking out the midday sun. A bell over the door bangs and subsides.

"Hano?" grouches Tartus.

"WHAT? JUST AS SECOND: CAN'T YOU TELL I'M BUSY?" Hano booms back.

Tartus bemused by this greeting.

"WHAT? ARE YOU JUST GOING TO STAND THERE? GIVE ME A HAND!" the giant voice from behind rows of abused antiques.

The three scramble around the coats, finding Hano engaged with a set of vacuum-sealed jars attached to a metal counter. A power drill lies at hand. "We could have used a set of these..." he says as they round a corner through the cast-offs.

"What are they?" asks Tihan.

"They're vacuum that holds in charge to these glass jars. You can run copper from them, strike quartz on iron and change the charge state."

"We always had enough quartz to go around." Tarnus smirks.

"Laugh if you want." Hano takes a quartz rock and smacks it against the iron counter, where a copper wire runs towards the jars.

The jars glow brightly for a moment. "They call them Leyden jars.

Oh... but we could have used these. Even with our own technologies. Remember how we found out about quartz's inherent electrical properties? We could never find a way to make it do anything though. Anyway, I'm having trouble getting some of our own things to work." "Our own things like what?" asks Tihan.

"Our glow lamps are dead; the light-beetles don't seem to like the environment," Hano bleats, slightly manic. "I believe I can get the quarts itself to illuminate with a little work. It's not how we think, we never would have figured it out. About some things these people here are quite clever."

"We use what they call tubes at the dig – they are immune to radiation, unlike the transistors in everything else made here," Tihan offers.

"We had research suggesting such things – but without uranium ore, we could never test even if we knew the element had to be there. At any rate, I was thinking of the return. We could use the quartz without having to resort to farming the light-beetles to light helmet lights, drilling light shafts through the mountains, only airshafts."

"Or instead of fussing with the quartz, we could make our own batteries like they have here," Tarnus says, enjoying needling Hano. It's always been what the mage responds to best.

"This is better. Yes, helmet lights would require a source of power for the excitation of the quartz – but imagine! We could illuminate most of Kragsteeth just by transitioning one water storage container. Evacuate a gas deposit and fill it with the component parts and cap it. Instant electricity. Like this but bigger."

"You would have a problem with regulation," Tihan critiques.

Hano momentarily crestfallen, brightens saying,"We could adjust the amount of metal slab in solution using a system of gears powered by the amount of electricity produced."

"That would work," Tihan agrees. "If we ever get back, if the accumulation..." Tihan says, but trails off.

"Which reminds me," says Tartus, breaking the thought train before they can get too upset. He takes the dark mead out of his rucksack.

"Where did you get those?" gasps Tarnus, taking one of the bottles.

"There's only two; you'll have to share."

"May I have one?" asks Hano. "For other purposes?"

Tartus looks back at the other two. "There's only one; you'll have to share." Tartus hands the other bottle to Hano.

"Have you been having any problems with your own things, not those from this place?" asks Hano.

Tartus says curtly,"I chipped my good axe."

"Hm," Hano says,"I'm worried our arrival is causing the breakdown of our things. The light-beetles dying from the dryness is one thing, chipped nurbinium is quite another. I can't figure out why."

Tarnus opens the bottle and hands it to Tihan. Tihan asks,

"Tartus you don't want any?" "Fenur has a whole case of them in his penthouse."

"A case?" says Hano. "Oh dear." "So how does this work?" Tihan asks Hano

Looking at the row of Leyden jars Hano contemplates,"I'm wondering if we could have used these as chargers to detonate the dark mead."

"Can you imagine the looks of the tall ones' if we had asked for that much of it? Enough to stop the accumulation at the base of Kragsteeth?" Tarnus asks rhetorically. He laughs.

"House and clan have gone to war over less," Tartus agrees.

"To make war for money..." Tarnus starts.

"We bought it from them," Tartus retorts.

"An old argument," says Hano, cutting them off,"And still many are dead."

"Please excuse our rudeness," offers Tartus.

Hano dismisses their exchange.

Tihan asks,"Do you get lonely here, Hano?"

"Yes. But also it is a quiet time to work on projects I have always thought about, but probably never would have gotten to," the mage dances around the question delicately. Of lighter skin and a different heritage, he was raised in the mountains, and has gone nearly papery here in the heat of the desert. To the three, the surplus store seems dark for an above ground abode, but to him it must be nearly as comfortable as the birds' nest city of Kragsteeth. An entire mountain carved from stone.

"About that..." starts Tartus.

Tihan scratches her beard.

"Yes?" "The accumulation..." he starts again.

Hano lifts bushy eyebrows, searching their faces.

Tihan picks up for Tartus,"We need you at the site. We may be... sensing them."

"The mountain ones were always... different-" begins Tihan.

"More advanced," corrects Tartus when he sees Hano's countenance start to close.

"Exactly," says Tarnus.

"-than the rest of us," continues Tihan. "Your people completed a major city first. The rule of law was first dictated there by the mages."

"And the development of other technologies took place first at Kragsteeth and Wind's Breath. We would expect nothing less than that those works would continue here," Tartus takes over before he can stop himself. Tihan has always been a favorite of the old mage. If she hadn't been female they would have adopted her into their clan and taught her as one of their own. On one of the rounds the mages made to the other cities of the underpeople, Hano had found her, and recommended her on her talent. Still the old ones were not ready to change. Tartus reflects that she would no longer be with them if she had been adopted into the Mage clan.

"My mother was married to one of the mage's apprentices, our clan is the same, even if our tribes are different, as we have talked of many times, Hano," Tihan says. "As an honor to my family, and for what could not be for me, please would you come to the site?"

Hano refuses to meet her gaze, examining instead every angle of his shop. "No." He continues after a moment,"Do you believe these two are worthy of you and your talents?"

Tartus grimaces, but says nothing.

"I have seen Tartus lead bravely on to a battlefield while the mages hid in their towers at Kragsteeth," Tihan says hotly.

Tarnus asks,"Is this what is left of the venerable mages of stone?"

The other two tense realizing Tarnus has gone too far.

"The accumulation found us? IMPOSSIBLE!" he explodes. "My kin made sure that-"

"We do not mean to disrespect the sacrifice of you or you clan. We feel lucky to have seen the wonder of Kragsteeth. Lucky for mages accepting us into their domain. However, what is, is."

"We would not have made the sacrifice if it could be undone. The transfer point is sealed from the other side. And I am the only one who could open it from this side."

"Which is why we wait for you to find us a way back, and why we also continue to look for another one." Tartus trying desperately to correct this minor disaster of diplomacy.

"Hano, you must come down to the site with us. You will see the truth of it," Tihan says. "The point of weakness between the worlds has moved from the old silver mines – t is being drawn by the uranium deposited at the dig."

"No. I have my projects and it is not possible. Even if they knew where to open it, they would not be able to."

"Unless one of the mages had been captured in the battle," Tartus nearly whispers, stopping conversation.

"We THOUGHT of this!" Hano rages. "You diggers never think above ground. We had to. The perspective was different from the top of the world. When we had hollowed out our mountains we had to look to other things. We had responsibilities! The population of Kragsteeth alone was greater than the population of the two other clans combined. When you came to us, we should have turned you away, and sacrificed you to the accumulation. Perhaps it would have been satisfied. We would have saved so many. No one of my kin would allow themselves to be captured and used in that way. Not after what happened to my city."

Tartus tries a last time, "The transfer point is extremely energetic and the possibility remains."

"You must go now, before I truly lose my temper. Go. Go on." Hano starts to shoo them and picks up the piece of quartz, waving it spastically. Tarnus takes the bottle of mead from Tihan, and takes a swig before handing it back as they are edged back towards the entrance to the surplus store, not really feeling any threat from the old mage swinging the rock. The old man following them with the quartz held out as a kind of talisman.

In the boiling heat of the midday sun, the door slams on them and they climb into the open air LRII.

"That could have gone worse," offers Tarnus. Tartus and Tihan turn and look at him. "Maybe not," he recasts the statement. Tartus starts the LRII.

13.

Fenur picks up a phone in the lobby. Out of a leather wallet he takes a business card with a shark fin on it, a number.

"Yeah, who's this?" "It's Fee." It nettles him, the shortening of his name.

"Hey, what's going on?"

"I'm looking for someone."

"Do I know this person?"

"We play poker sometimes." A pause. "Meet me at the diner I go to."

"Time?"

"I eat late, maybe two o'clock?"

"It can't be a social call. I've got to get some sleep; I go on at ten," Fenur shorter than he likes with the Finn.

"I understand. See you then, ok? And Fee, lighten up, man.

Life is supposed to be fun."

Fenur hangs up, checks his watch, there being no clocks in the hotel, and walks to his private elevator door past replicas of ancient gods unfamiliar to him.

He showers and redresses in what people refer to as street clothes, and heads back out. He parks at a shop he hunts for vinyl records at, deciding to walk the few blocks to the Finn's hang out.

A pre-fab art deco diner is recovering from 2:00am "lunch" rush, the wait staff helping the bus staff to clear tables. Fenur finds a table at the rear in a corner, sitting towards the door. The Finn, had he arrived first, wouldn't have chosen the last table in the corner, but Fenur doesn't worry about this kind of thing; he's fast and agile enough it's unimportant.

Twenty minutes later the Finn ducks in, a felt hat with an upturned brim on his balding head. He wears a leather jacket even in the heat. Fenur finds it distasteful that people have so much and that they still wear animal hide. Where he's from, it was necessary; here it is not.

The Finn sits with a look over his shoulder.

"Alright, I'm here," he says.

"Where's Norvil?" asks Fenur.

"What? No 'thanks for the job'? No, 'nice to see you' or 'how's Lou doing'? Nothing?" the Finn grins.

Fenur waits patiently.

"Truth is, I don't know."

"You always know something."

"I heard some things," the Finn grimaces and rocks his head side to side. "But really like, he could have been abducted by aliens for what I heard, and that would make as much sense. You know what I mean?"

"What have you heard?"

"Our guy, Sato - no Hideki Irabu by the way, if what you two did is any indication - he says some guys showed up, boom, boom boom, no more Norvil. And Stephen is freaking out about his hotel."

"Sato said something that was intelligible?"

"He kind of mimed it out."

"And no one was aware of what was happening?" Fenur slightly incredulous. "Where was this?"

"It was at the hotel."

"So it wasn't what you asked me to do with him? With Sato?" asks Fenur, trying to push down a feeling of thousands of years of history the Finn can't possibly understand.

"We had our yak put up there at the hotel. He said they just up and grabbed Norvil in the lobby. Stuffed him in a limo." The Finn shrugs noncommittally. "Has the feel of pros. I asked Sato, but he couldn't identify them."

"Have you talked to him?" Fenur indicates the owner of the hotel, Stephen.

"He doesn't fraternize with the other side." The Finn flashes his teeth in a grin.

Fenur absorbs this. "The poker game off then?"

"Hah. You wish. I gotta win some of that money back, my man." And the Finn slaps his hands on the table in a drumming motion upsetting water glasses, the table and silverware to jumping.

"Anything else in Sato's mime?" Fenur probes.

"Sato's about as useful when it comes to stuff like that as you are in a bar fight. He's not saying everything he knows, but that's fine. We all have our separate business." The Finn waves off further talk of what this business might be.

"Ok." Fenur lets it go.

The Finn puts two hundred down on the table. Fenur stands. "Finn, you don't owe me anything."

"The money is for the food."

"Ok, but I got to go," Fenur says. "And I didn't order anything."

"And the info," says the Finn.

"I didn't give you any info," Fenur responds.

"That's what you think," quips the Finn, continuing,"And a little bit back for the job."

Fenur nods to the Finn, trying not to feel self-conscious about the body movement, the movement feels so strange to him. "You need to partner Sato with anyone again, come to me."

"I didn't get the feeling you two hit it off so great," the Finn offers.

Fenur ignoring this statement. "It's business. It works for us. Doesn't have to be personal."

"Everything is personal. Could you not loom over me like that, man? I gotta eat. Now get outta here." The Finn laughs at his own joke.

14.

And Hano said he wouldn't help?" asks one of the miners.

"He says it can't be happening," Tartus says matter-of-factly, not leaving any room for argument.

The group of miners have gathered in a common area of the trailer park for campfire building and grilling. It's in the open, but other than the dig, it's the place that feels most like home. Smells of food, central fire, their own kind.

Tihan shoves her hands in pockets and clamps her lips together, keeping quiet, which Tarnus appreciates. She's angry but waits while the murmur erupts.

"That's what they said before!"

"When we showed up at their doors, having fought their battle for them-"

"-I lost my entire family to their willful ignorance, and now to-"

"-He's the only one left, how can he not see-"

"-will we ever find peace? If we couldn't escape the accumulation by crossing, how-"

Tartus puts out his hands, holding them up for quiet. The shift has just ended, and the miners arrived back at the camp. Tarnus says quietly next to Tartus,"They are tired and dirty, and haven't seen a bed in nearly twenty hours There's nothing to be resolved."

Tartus giving approbation, listening. "There is nothing more we can do today. Find a bed and rest. We will find an answer."

"How long have you been saying that there is an answer to this deadlock? We believed the mages. And now they refuse to help. And you. What can you really do?" says someone. Tartus is disheartened to find he still has trouble remembering the digger's name, despite memories of his accomplishments. The name comes to him. "Morno, you must take care of your physical needs first Rest and recuperate.

Have a beer and a shower. Sit at the fire. It is something we did not have for so many years before. We must take advantage of it while we can, if we mus confront the accumulation again."

Somewhat placated, Morno grimaces but agrees.

"How could they be crossing? Did Hano even say that much?"

"No. He emphatically said that it was impossible. He alluded to a project h had been working on he needed time to finish. So have heart."

Tihan says lowly to Tarnus,"He didn't say anything about it having to do with our predicament."

"Let him talk, it's working," Tarnus replies.

"We're out of nurbinium. We have only what weapons we could carry The mages were mostly subsumed in the crossing. We cannot win this fight someone who looks more focused than those coming off-shift says.

"The houses across the city have more stores, and were able to get mor through than we were."

"By virtue of the fact that they went first," someone says bitterly.

"And other factors," adds someone else. A statement so rancorous the crowd's temper immediately flares: meaning luck, meaning beauty and the ease of a life with it, meaning their own desire as good hosts to accommodate. Tarnus not stepping in as mediator between Tartus and the clans – part of his role as Tartus' second is letting the crowd, or even the diplomats from the houses, burrow as it will.

Tihan speaks up, saying,"The mages demanded that we defend them, it was part of the treaty-"

"You speak for the mages, a voice I grow tired of," replies another voice from the crowd. A miner named Nusmo. One of Morno's fellow clansmen – Hano's clansmen as well. However, they were not from Kragsteeth, which is what separates them from the mage. Interclan politics a bottomless morass.

"You grow tired of the voices who took you in when you were about to be exterminated?" asks a voice with a mountain accent. Morno again.

"We must not fall to this bickering. Look what happened to the mountain clan-"

"THAT WAS NOT OUR FAULT. IF YOU HAD DEALT WITH YOUR OWN PROBLEMS WE NEVER WOULD HAVE-"

"The mountain people: always the same. Shove your superiority in a hole and cover it, Morno."

The crowd erupts as Morno shoves his way out, followed by a few others.

"Please don't leave," Tartus asks.

"None of the mountain clan are represented in the leadership here!" shouts one of the ones shoving their way out. Nusmo again. "You are inexperienced and young, and we protect you as our own.

We are imploring you: do not leave the parley," Tarnus shouts.

"Inexperienced?" the last one of them shouts. "We who have lived through more than any of our kin before us? Who lost our elders, our city, and all of our ways? You dare-"

"We tell you what you do not want to hear out of respect. As kin. What would you do instead? Where would you go?" asks Tarnus, Tartus letting him play the enforcer.

The younger one, Morno, at the back glares at him, and turns and leaves.

Tartus climbs to the roof of the Airstream using the aluminum ladder. The top of the aluminum-domed trailer is slick, but his heavy rubber-soled boots act as stoppers against sliding.

He lights a cigar with a Zippo and lays back, puffing, legs squished as counterbalancing spring against falling off. The aluminum roof cold against his back.

How often has he as king had a moment alone? Not since exploring cave breakthroughs in his youth has he found peace. How often since their arrival here? A few moments without Tarnus shepherding every conversation, or Tihan's need of signings, confirmations, machinations, to keep the clans from splintering. And then the houses. And Fenur.

Around the glow of the cigar ember he looks up at the stars in different formations. Here they have names for the arrangements – a quaint custom those from underground would never have thought of. The houses have nothing like it as far as he knows. Some of the stars he suspects are the same – seven over there in a different arrangement from home. As though maybe he sees them from a different angle now. Or if he squints and looks deep, some of those distant places the mages studied, that he remembers from his own education, or the smudges against the deeper black which extend from horizon to horizon. He wishes he had a painting from home, or could remember the cartography of it better-

"-It was Norton at the well of ice. Not you."

"If only we could have mediated the contract earlier between the houses and the clans, we would not have had to look so far from the mines."

"The clans did not have enough power in the negotiations. You were not engaged with the digging-"

"My family wanted me educated, do not bring your issues between-"

"I did not mean to give offense, I only suggest that without your presence on the exploration the clans would have been taken completely unaware."

Voices from below Tartus. He crawls to the edge of the Airstream and looks over. Morno and another of his clan talking. "If we could have gone to the other clans, to the mages and showed them…" Morno thinking outloud, speaking to Nusmo,"But there wasn't time. I joined with the expedition, but we expected no movement on the politics between the houses and clans."

"The mages were not interested in any thoughts but their own," scoffs the other. "They wanted the mead. They wanted not to have to provide the oil to the houses. Arrogance."

"We should not have been so far in the north," Morno says.

Tartus can see how regret twists in him.

"And where else would you have looked for volcanism? To take more on the expedition, simply would have meant a quicker start to the accumulation." Tartus wonders why they don't smell the cigar. It must be drifting up and away. They must think he's inside.

"I should apologize to him. He is right of course. To hide the mage. To keep us separate from the houses. But the..."

The other blocks Morno's way to the door of the Airstream. "He is arrogant and indifferent. If there had been another would we be living like this? Would we not be living more as the houses live?" The other's name is Nusmo. Tartus frustrated at himself for not being able to remember the clanmember's name during the parley. He is unsurprised at their anger, and also angry with himself, seeing his inability to remember the name as an indicator of the salience of what Nusmo says.

"Leave it. Perhaps you should contact the houses for assistance?" Nusmo asks.

"They are in turmoil. But what could they do? It was unlucky – what they found. They keep secrets and blame themselves."

"What has he done?" Nusmo asks about Tartus, adding,"If our own king were here, what would he do? What would your kindred say? With their ancient connections to the houses."

A thought Tartus has had as well. The following through of this thought has not gone in the positive direction Nusmo seems to have found.

Morno turns and walks towards his own residence. "I will wait. Perhaps you are right. Perhaps I should speak with Norton."

Tartus repositions himself on the roof, irritated that a moment alone has turned into intrigue. Feeling guilty that his people are so unhappy and that he must keep watch on young the two younger diggers.

15.

Late morning light through the shutters of the Airstream; Tartus comes awake to it sneaking in past the blinds. He hears shouting outside and raises himself up trying to straighten creaky body and hair flattened on one side. Hair and beard soaked from drool. The shouts angry past the insulating walls of the trailer.

He creeps to the door in boxers and a gray tank, looking out a window, refusing to get involved this early; long ago he learned that most of it would resolve itself, and what wouldn't, would wait. Plus, a punch in the head first thing in the morning is a terrible way to start the day. When he sees what it is he rushes to open the door.

"-KIN KILLER!"

"How dare you invade our camp!"

"Where's Tartus?" shouts Fenur, swinging a fold-up picnic chair left over from the ill-fated parley of last night, encircled by half a dozen shorter camp members, mainly mountain people as Tartus takes a quick head count.

"I'm up," says Tartus. "Leave him be."

"We can handle this," says one of the mountain folk.

"Apparently. But I asked him to come," Tartus lies. Fenur looks at him, supporting the statement.

The six of the mountain clan begin to back off.

"Come on in," says Tartus, brushing sand and stones from his hardened but still bare feet as he steps back on to the aluminum steps of the Airstream.

Boxer shorts and t-shirt, wild hair and desert forming – paradoxically - an image of power to Fenur. Fenur drops the chair without looking at it, after double-checking the other six, and steps up brisk and elegant, still in the previous night's tuxedo.

"I think this is the first time one of you has visited our encampment."

Fenur confirms this by body language.

Tartus raises bushy eyebrows, wiping sleep from his eyes, and turns to the galley to make coffee. As he bangs around in cabinets slightly out of reach, Fenur says,"The mead is gone."

Tartus stops for a second considering. "When?"

"Last night while I was at work."

Tarnus in the doorway with Tihan, saying,"You bring good tidings!" Fenur turns and greets the sarcasm. Tarnus continues, explaining their arrival,"We heard the commotion and then saw the car. We figured we better find our way over."

Tartus running water and grinding beans.

"Make enough for everyone," Tihan commands Tartus, and flops on a sprung built-in couch, which always remains in the down position. Tartus endorses the idea by pouring more ground beans, chewing on morning dry mouth.

Fenur looks surprised at them drinking coffee.

"I don't think it was us," he says, referring to the missing dark mead. "We had a parley between clans last night, and I don't think anyone was obviously missing."

"Of course we can't really ask them either. Without letting them know of its existence," Tarnus offers, lounging in the doorway.

Fenur continues to duck to miss the ceiling, finally says to Tihan,"May I?" indicating space on the couch, incongruity considering the setting. Tihan gives the closest thing to a giggle either of the other two has heard from her.

"But of course..." she gestures magnanimously. Fenur sits next to her, legs crossed and back straight. Tarnus watches, scratching his head, fingers disappearing into the nappy burlap surrounding his skull, appearing nonplussed.

"We have to assume one of ours took it," Tartus says.

"How would they have found out? No one works at the hotel-" Tihan offers.

"And no one but Tartus talks to the houses," finishes Tarnus.

Fenur grimaces. "I work with a few people outside of the hotel, but I don't know how they would have found out. Or why they would want it, even if they understood what it was."

Tartus gives him a questioning look while he waits for the coffee.

"They frequent the high-end card games."

"Bookies?" "And their associates," Fenur responds.

Tartus laughs. "This is what you've been hiding?"

Tarnus slightly bewildered by the depths of Fenur's pathos at hiding such a thing; the three of them loving to gamble.

"Associating with locals..."

"It's not so bad," Tihan says kindly.

"He's finally learned to gamble. Good on him," Tarnus says as aside to her.

"Still it could lead to trouble. Could a member of one of the houses figure out what to do with the mead?" Tartus asks posing an unknowable hypothetical. The others make gestures: the mine is deep, the next load could be the motherload; or: you never know what the next vein is.

"From my experience, no," laughs Fenur darkly.

"Would it even work for them?" wonders Tihan. "It's difficult enough for one of the mages to focus it. And a local would probably just drink it-"

"Halfwits..." Tarnus cavils.

"And our ways of making and working are different," Tihan adds.

"The houses would have difficulty."

"It worked for the accumulation. And they had none of their own life essence. We were wrong to underestimate that," Tarnus rumbles.

"Can you ask them?" Tartus continues on the thought.

Fenur offers one of his peoples' mannerisms that the diggers associate with a negative response. "Not easily. How would I explain why bottles of mead are important? Even if I could... would they be honest with me? I doubt it. Only Leanor and Norton understand it really."

Tartus grabs mugs and fills them. "You must try. And we will look here and at the site. Perhaps one of the mountain folk..."

"Tartus!" Tihan says, shocked. He grimaces, but continues passing out coffee.

"Look at what they just tried. We must be honest, if this is to work. Everyone is aware of the inter-clan strife. Not only among our own kind and his. Between the clans. Between the houses of the tall ones. It's how we got here. Can you honestly say you believe the mountain folk are not capable of stealing the mead for their own ends? Believing their actions would help?" he looks at her from under bushy eyebrows, and sips the coffee. She refuses to answer.

"I see I'm not the only one with a weakness for certain of the local's charms," says Fenur, trying to break the tension, gestures at the mugs of coffee.

Tartus, relieved to be off the subject says,"Tihan saw it in town. We ascertained that the cafe was like a tavern and decided to try it one night out of desperation and boredom," Tarnus offers. He sips. "Good. We didn't sleep afterward. At the time it was bad – since... it has it charms. Especially when rotating to swing shift."

"You had a parley last night?" Fenur tiptoes, returning to Tihan's previous statement.

Tartus offers a brusque affirmation, dismissing camp politics.

"Leanor has called the gathering of the houses today. A convention room. As the last remaining member of my house, I am asking you to represent me in the gathering," Fenur offers with no discernible expression, by way of explaining why he has shown up this morning.

Tartus leans against the upward sloping wall of the Airstream, not needing to duck forward. He sips the coffee and thinks while the other two exchange glances. Tartus laughs. "Of course."

"Tartus..." Tarnus warns about the involvement in house affairs.

"It will be mayhem," offers Tihan. "One of us representing the Far Sea people," a deep laugh ruminating and then escaping from somewhere inside. "What I love about the locals," Tihan says. "Is they will think we are playful versions of them."

"No, they won't," scoffs Tarnus.

"Yes, they will," says Tihan, a mirthful but flinty glint in her eye.

"I will bet you money they won't."

"Money it is then."

16.

"Is there anything in particular you want from them?" Tartus asks on the ride over.

"To stop bullying me. I have one last vial of oil. As far as I know no others possess any. They want it. I want them to leave me alone." Fenur's frustration at the continuance of the houses' old behavior showing through even his normally dispassionate mien.

"Still, it continues, despite promises and treaties..." Tarnus expressing his vexation amongst friends before the need for statesmanship.

"Bullies never stop. They just get better at hiding it," Fenur responds from his perch in the back seat of the LRII, the desert air whirling around him.

People move through the hotel, off on mid-evening adventures. Rooms for gambling breathe, emitting a low emphysema like wet rasp in glowing light. Those in the lobby ignore them, or watch impassively. The tall ones arrive by limo, or on foot, springing lightly from the inter-hotel shuttles and tram. Some dress in evening wear, some dressed in rarer materials.

Tartus stands with Fenur in the lobby watching the arrivals.

Fenur attracts little attention from the locals in his tuxedo, but Tartus has chosen his ceremonial greaves and axe - the axe strapped to his back in the old tradition.

"Look at them," Fenur says, barely able to hide his contempt.

"We all must play our parts," Tartus quietly, thunder in the distance, but equally worried.

A sign at one of the convention doors says: WELCOME: 'PEOPLE FROM ANOTHER WORLD'!

A stylized version of the local's fanciful creature called a dragon on the sign, emitting flames from its mouth.

Off to one side visible through the door of a bar Tarnus and Tihan wait in street clothes, drinking tonic water. Tartus considers the bottling of a gas-filled spring to be one of the locals' greatest inventions. Why had they never thought of it with the rivers underground? Good stuff.

"I love your costume," says a woman in a pantsuit walking by, carrying a shopping bag with the logo of a store from inside the hotel.

"Thank you," Tartus says while Fenur tries not to laugh. Inside the bar the other two are exchanging rowdy handshake congratulations over their bet. Money changes hands. Tihan holds up the money to Tartus. Tarnus trying to take it back. Tartus scowls at them.

The doors to the convention room open and one of Leanor's staff emerges carrying the crystal bell saved from the veldt.

"What was his name again," asks Tartus clearly blanking. "His name? Konor," Fenur returns, searching briefly for it in his memory. "You wouldn't know much of him. Though you've heard the story of how they – and your clansmen Morno - found the accumulation." Tartus confirms this with a grunt. There behind him one of the other characters in that story, Leanor's father, Norton.

Leanor having arranged this convention at her hotel.

"It could have happened to any of us," Tartus says.

"The finding of the accumulation? Yes... But it happened to him. If Norton were king..." Fenur stops, realizing Tartus goes tense at the ponderance. Fenur doesn't want to make him, as king of the underpeople, uncomfortable. They watch Norton shuffling to find a seat.

Konor finishes checking the lobby, and finds the count to his satisfaction. He rings the bell.

The lobby stops and goes quiet for a moment. Even the tourists stop and look.

"Call to the chosen. Call to the original ones. Call from your original forests, mountains and seas. Return now."

The tallest in the lobby, immaculate, part ways from the others, the locals, and move into the convention room. Waking, the locals return to their amble towards parts unknown.

As they walk through into the convention room, Fenur says,"It seems ridiculous to leave the seas section in for one person. They never even believed we were a true house."

"That is why you wanted me to speak on your behalf," Tartus offers, as they make their way to the doors of the convention room. "You can't let what happened allow them to control this. Stay quiet unless I ask you a specific question." Fenur, indifferent at the suggestion, says nothing.

At the door Konor stops them. "He may not enter," He says to Fenur, meaning Tartus.

Tartus, taking Konor's hand from his chest where he has been stopped, says,"Under the treaty of Wind's Breath you must admit all those with just cause."

Konor refuses to drop his hand from Tartus' grasp,"And what cause might that be?" still looking at Fenur.

"Something which concerns us all."

"You must prove this before-"

"Because of the accumulation, this is not the agreement that was reached. Let me pass. Or do you mean to cause affront to a king of the underpeople? Do you risk open war in this foreign land? I will explain all in due course." Tartus' other hand reaches behind him, resting on the axe hilt. Fenur tense to the point of quivering.

Konor considers, looks at the placement of Tartus' hand, and lets them through into the sumptuous meeting room. Flowers line the walls, crystal hangs from the ceiling. A stage and velvet curtains outlining Leanor's place. Her throne saved, carried, up until the end, by the people of the Far Seas. It sits center stage.

"It feels exactly like a tree home," Tartus says under his breath to Fenur before he can stop himself.

Chairs set too close together by hotel staff are rearranged by those slightly too long for them. Years of tradition, but not courtesy, keep them from commenting or staring as Fenur and Tartus walk to seats near the front.

Leanor alone at the front of the room, standing on the third step of a small dais erected in her honor, two of the old honor guard standing on either side of her on the second step.

The conventioneers exchanging looks as Tartus approaches.

"We bid you welcome, Tartus of the underpeople," Leanor says, following the established protocol, if somewhat frostily.

"Thank you, queen," returns Tartus,"But I am here on behalf of the remaining of the house of the Far Sea. Not for myself or my people."

Leanor flashes a brittle smile, looking briefly at Fenur. "You seek an advocate on your behalf?"

"He seeks an advocate on behalf of all the people of the Far Sea." Tartus restrains Fenur from talking by putting a hand on his forearm.

"Of which there remains only one."

"One here in this land, but this is a convention of all of your peoples. And their respective houses." He corrects himself from using his own people's colloquialism of clans, before it slips out. They always speak in English now, a small safety precaution; the words clan and house nearly identical in their own languages, though the connotations are different. Making the transition into

English is one more round in an already murky game of diplomacy. "The one on this side from the house of Nur requests representation. It is his place to speak for the others given past events, and their inability to be here at this time." This is the only indication Tartus gives that he is willing to go as far as is necessary for the situation to be resolved in his favor.

"Do you expect that the others survived-" Leanor stops herself abruptly. Others of the houses stop and stare for a moment before returning to settling in. Gathering herself together she says,"Of course. We bid you both welcome."

The situation seemingly resolved, Konor resumes with the standard protocol ascending to the first step of the platform. Konor begins,"We will first take any house business."

"That's somewhat truncated," Fenur whispers.

Tartus agrees, waiting on the edge of the dais, feeling Fenur discharging equal parts cool hatred and nervous apprehension from beside him. Since the queen did not offer them a seat they stand to one side of the dais waiting.

Someone behind them offers up house business:"The house of Vil is owed a large sum of local money by the people of the forests-" Turns to see Vilhan, the third member of the party that discovered the accumulation marching through the doors and towards his proper place as king. Leanor holding the real power as the line of succession goes through her. He climbs the stage, and stands in his place behind her.

Tartus ignoring this small play on Vilhan's part to interject himself into the situation – he has never been comfortable with his subordinate role as Leanor's mate.

Konor from lower on the dais stops this by sharply interjecting,"The house of Nor will address this matter in due course. Any business of import?" Vilhan goes red as he takes his seat in a smaller chair than the throne behind the still standing Leanor.

"Tartus what progress by the Mage?" someone from the back asks.

Tartus turns, looking... ...finds a face he remembers fighting alongside with at the battle of the pass. He makes a large negative body gesture. "We cannot get an answer from him."

"Leanor, why did the remaining Mage not receive an invitation?" queries someone older, off to the side of the podium, with a full head of short silver hair. Tartus glad to be at the front and able to see over the sea of heads. Norton, Leanor's father, the questioner.

"We sent an invitation via the underpeople's encampment, as they keep him safe in hiding," she states, turning the brittle smile back on Tartus again.

"This is the first I have heard of it," says Tartus, feeling Fenur stiffen.

"It was delivered to Morno," says Konor.

Tartus makes a mental note about the last member of the band that had made the initial exploration that found the accumulation.

They hadn't really realized what would come of it. Or how fast it would happen.

"Is there any progress?" the same older voice asks from the middle of the crowd to Tartus left. Norton again.

Leanor frozen by this breach of protocol.

"No. None that he would speak of last time I was with him." Tartus continues to look at Leanor, and make eye contact, waiting for the eruption which leaves the room dissolving in the noise of people's daily lives and the desire for interruption, return, a change from what they have become.

Leanor holding up her hands for calm.

"We had need of our own-"

"But they were unavailable," Leanor cuts off this line of thinking.

"Unavailable? They were subsumed into the accumulation."

The older voice again," We cannot dwell like this on our personal grievances and what could have been."

"Father..." Leanor says, less formally. The older one stops.

"Despite everything, he's right," another says.

"How can we-" Leanor waits, and continues to smile, a mask meaning nothing. Tartus sensing Fenur vibrating to the point of not being able to contain himself as the conversation continues around the queen. The interjection from Norton, her father, having rattled her. Tartus looks for an easy escape from the lower step of the dais where they have been trapped by Konor loose handling of the gathering.

"Where is Norvil?" asks Vilhan, bored and somewhat absent.

"Vilhan of the plains peoples, I COMMAND YOU TO BE SILENT," Leanor says, letting go of her composure suddenly. Underneath a wall of rage can be seen and felt by Tartus, before Leanor locks it away again and he decorum returns. Quiet descends on the gathering. "And what do the sea people require of me?" she asks turning to Tartus.

Tartus opens his mouth, knowing how hopeless it is after her outburst, when a disturbance at the entry to the convention room stops him. Konor descends from the stage towards police gathered at the door. He confers with them while the room waits.

"Leanor, Vilhan, you are needed outside." Konor hesitates, then adds,"And Fenur."

Stuck, Leanor composes herself and descends the stage, walking out of the room, followed by Vilhan, Fenur and a trailing Tartus.

Outside locals wait. A crowd is gathering.

Three uniformed police and two out of uniform, in suits, wait for the small group of conventioneers.

"Leanor Forest?" says one of the men wearing a suit.

"Yes?" asks Leanor.

"We believe we have found your brother, Norvil? He's your brother right?"

"Yes," she stops him.

"He has been missing? He was reported missing."

Leanor turns and looks back at her father, Norton, turned around in his seat watching. He stands and walks to the door. "Norvil is my son," he says when the police look at him.

"Could both of you come with us?" asks one of the uniforms. The relative oddity of the gathering passing observed but unsaid between these local officials.

"We may have found him, but we're sorry... ...he didn't make it," adds one of the locals in the blue uniforms.

Leanor's composure cracks and she leans on Fenur, her head against his neck as she starts to cry. Vilhan discomfited by this. Fenur doesn't acknowledge her, but as she sobs, finally lets his guard down and strokes her hair. "Forgive me, Fenur." She uses the familiar possessive of the old language. "Forgive us all."

"There is nothing you could have done, Lea," he murmurs in the other direction, the interaction at odds with his formal body stance. His eyes dance around looking for escape.

"Please come with us?" she asks Fenur, who follows impassively.

"Vilhan?" she asks.

"Of course, my-" Vilhan stops himself, a formality he chops off abruptly.

"The people of the plains have always been such good friends," says Norton trying to find a political way through the awkwardness of Leanor choosing Fenur over Vilhan publicly in a time of need.

The police exchange looks, and wait while the small group collects itself at the news. The others in the convention room, realizing what is happening begin to talk amongst themselves, slowly rising from the rows of tightly spaced chairs.

Tartus and Fenur exchange a look, as the group departs. Tartus turns towards Tihan and Tarnus at the bar.


17.


They arrive by ones and twos, or sometimes as a small group. Never more than a few at a time. The parking attendant sees v twins, elegant sedans with drivers. The high-end passenger cars carry immaculately clothed, beautiful people who move with a gravity and presence reserved for royalty.

Wreaths of blue oil smoke emerge from indestructible but unpleasant looking vehicles which spill short ugly people onto the sidewalk or the cement of the garage where they try and disentangle hair and body parts from each other, what they rode in on, grab rucksacks off back bench seats and de-bungie from sissy bars.

The two groups seem to know each other and sometimes acknowledge the others, but it is a sober occasion and no one speaks.

In the lobby and waiting rooms, there: Konor and Morno in a corner conversing in low tones. One gesticulating with voice down, while the other makes affirmative motions, arms crossed. There: another group of the shorter types drinking coffee, scratching beards, looking for someone in authority to speak with. A few of the taller, well-put-together types weeping. Some looking uncomfortable. Or angry.

Tartus, Tihan and Tarnus holding up a hospital wall, waiting for sight of Fenur and Leanor, and for the rest of the identification process to unfold. Through doors they see Fenur, Leanor and her father, Norton. Leanor leans on

Fenur. Police take notes, and forms are handed back and forth. Norton nodding in the way of the locals. The police accepting this frippery he adds on to his body language. Making the locals more at home in their own environment. Making them seem less different from those who belong here.

In front of the doors stands Vilhan allowing the immediate family, plus Fenur, privacy during the identification, holding the two groups of refugees away from the legal proceedings, as they try and see what is going on through the doors, or offer help to those speaking with the authorities in seclusion. An odd look to Vilhan's countenance.

"I hope he's not thinking about..." Tihan starts, watching Fenur with Leanor through a window in the double swinging doors at the end of the hallway.

"Ti, he got forced into playing nursemaid again. That's all," Tarnus says.

Tartus says nothing, watching grief unfold. Watching the room, worried having so many of their kind so close together with the others. Tartus says finally,"I don't think there have been this many of us together since Wind's Breath."

"The scouting from the tunnels after," Tarnus offers.

"Yes..." Tartus exhales. "Old silver mines," Tihan says. "So much of it." "And no nurbinium," Tartus responds.

"No wonder the mages were attracted to the opening. And the tall ones. Their pendants."

Tartus agrees, not knowing what else to say.

"With the scouting missions and finding the city... and uranium. So much is different," Tihan wonders.

"Did you see the shop? Hano getting sold solid silver dinnerware sets-"

"Keep your voice down about where he is," Tartus says quietly to Tarnus.

"Imagine. Eating off of it. Like it was nothing. To have that much it."

"Nurbinium's rare enough for my taste," Tihan says.

"Nothing too rare," Tarnus says, the old mine joke, trying to raise their spirits. He gets nothing more than slightly upturned lips from the other two.

A lull descends on the lobby as people wait.

Fenur, Leanor and Norton finished with the police. Vilhan looks up from his post near the swinging doors as they walk past him. He falls in behind them.

Leanor stops in the middle of the room, Fenur now off to one side. "Thank you for joining us. And to our other friends as well. It is so good to see you again. The first time since our time together in the mountains when you took us in. It is kind of you to come and express your concern. Sad that we should meet again under such circumstances," she pauses gathering herself up,"My brother, the one who was known as Norvil, is dead. I have seen him."

Looks are exchanged among the two groups.

"Thank you for being here," she ends heavily, and seems to visibly shrink. She returns to Fenur and her father. Vilhan stands to one side controlling the crowd as people begin to press in, to say small things, to ask small things, to offer condolences, to wonder to each other what has happened.

"...murdered..."

"How..."

"...to die so far from home..."

Fingers meet small vials of the remaining precious oil, the different houses making small washing motions as they coat their hands.

The shorter ones pushing by, not throwing their customary elbows, which tends to get people out of the way, also offering sincerest regrets.

To one side a scuffle breaking the somber mood.

Konor's fist connects with Morno' nose. Morno offers an animal grunt. Everyone stops and turns with an intake of breath, stunned, waiting for Morno to make the next move.

"It's alright," Morno says, rubbing his nose and finding a little blood on the back of his hand. "It's nothing. The same altercation as always amongst friends. We argue over who assigns themselves too much fault for finding the accumulation." Morno motioning it away.

The group seems visibly relieved, and the moment passes. Some look at Norton.

Tarnus says under his breath,"You would think after all of this time they would have decided where fault lies."

"Or both would have decided they should be exchanging blows with Norton," Tihan offers.

"Imagine how it would have been," Tarnus says darkly. Watching the two groups carefully, so no one hears, Tarnus says sardonically,"The oldest of the three houses? It could never have been Norton's fault."

"And yet he is not king," reflects Tartus.

"And Leanor is queen," Tihan offers as rebuttal.

"It would have been civil war if he had not been able to marry Leanor and Vilhan. The houses would have warred over the death of Vilhan's brother on the expedition. And the responsibility for the enslavement of the people of the Far Seas lies on his brother's shoulders as well."

"They were truly twins. Ugliness in both of them," Tarnus speaking plainly to Tartus, as he often does in his role as interlocutor.

"A civil war - we would not have lasted as long as we did against the accumulation. It would have been outright slaughter. None of us would be here – or anywhere - now." Tartus subsides for a moment. "Vilhan and Vilhon. You are right of course Tarnus; and Norton is known to me mainly by his choice of companions." Tartus finishes his thought,"The other houses were forced to choose incompetence over divisiveness."

Tarnus and Tihan raise bushy eyebrows at such a bald statement from Tartus.

Something happening at the entrance to the hospital. A long foreign limousine stopping and a chauffeur rounding the side to open a door. Three men disgorged.

Through the doors a man in an expensive suit, two more dressed like him. One carries a narrow leather-bound briefcase.

"It's the owner," Tartus hears Fenur say in a low voice, the three standing close to the family group.

Stephen ascends a short flight of stairs past a reception and admission desk to the lobby.

The crowd parts slightly to let the three men through.

"Leanor," Stephen says,"I'm so sorry to hear of your loss."

It takes her a moment to recover. "Thank you, Stephen." The other two men say nothing.

"I didn't know you kept such interesting and varied company," Stephen says looking around the room at the motley assortment.

"Norvil's things." One of the men proffers the briefcase. Fenur takes it.

"I wanted to personally offer my condolences and bring you Norvil's few personal items. He was hard to get to know, but we very much enjoyed his time in our company."

Tartus boggles at how convoluted the statement is. "Little kings..." he mutters to the other two, who concur, making little gestures going mostly unnoticed around them.

An awkward pause while Leanor considers the man the way she might consider an insect invading her queenly sanctuary.

"He had so many friends," Stephen rushes to fill the void.

"He did," says Norton.

Stephen says,"Well, please let us know if there is anything we can do for you."

"Thank you, Stephen," says Leanor.

Stephen turns and retreats through the front door to the waiting limo.

Leanor gathers herself up again. "Friends, we will resume the convention to tomorrow. Until then." She makes her way through the small crowd accompanied by Fenur.


18.


"You must return to the hospital, Fenur. You must obtain Norvil's pendant of life," Norton says in low tones. They occupy various positions in Leanor's suite. A view of castle turrets from the panoramic window.

"Send one of your own, people, Norton," Fenur rejoins,"The house of No should collect their own things."

"Whatever your feelings on what happened... my daughter..." Norton stops. He is older and has always been taciturn in the way of some in the older generations. Fenur had never liked him. The internal machinations of the houses after the unleashing of the accumulation had kept him from being king but he has never asked anything of Fenur before, Fenur realizes. Strange Norton lost so much and has never tried to exert any real authority. "My daughter still loves you. Whatever is between you, there is also that. You are the only one she considers reliable," he stops. "And I agree."

Fenur considers his awkward position. He walks to where Leanor sits on a leather couch. "I am returning to the hospital to retrieve Norvil's pendant of life," he says close to her ear. She looks up at him, regal despite the strain. She gives him a small body signal of commanding affirmation, which irks him. Quickly, he changes tone, saying to her,"If you wish, you may have another perform the task."

"No," she says. "I would like it to be you." She looks out at the castle turrets. "Please," she says stiffly, barely acknowledging him.

He turns and leaves, angry.

After changing into non-descript clothes, a pair of jeans and a blue t-shirt (it's amazing how much of the time he spends in the tuxedo) and parking a block away, Fenur walks towards a side entrance to the hospital, trying not to give off the air of someone doing reconnaissance. At the outside drop-off point for non-emergency care, he changes direction, walking across a busy five lane street to a minimart which sits at a diagonal from the mammoth hospital.

Most of the hospital is underground, built into the earth like one of Tartus, Tihan, and Tarnus' dwellings.

The identification room was next to the morgue, a low point in the hospital and next to a garage housing employee cars and ambulances. Three larger pay garages sit at various ends of the hospital structure.

Realizing there is no easy way into the lower levels of the hospital where they had seen Norvil's body, he opts for the most direct course. He takes out his keys, and opens a soda he obtained at the minimart. He hates the stuff. Smelling it, he wonders again how the locals drink it. He takes one swig to prime his breath with the sugary stink of it as he walks past the watered sod on a city sidewalk. He turns at an entrance to the employee parking and starts down a ramp into the underbelly area of the hospital. Once inside, he takes another swig of the soda, swinging his car keys for effect. Hide in plain sight: it's the first thing they learned here. A truck descends the same ramp he just walked down, turns and starts to back up making a cautionary beep as it advances backwards towards a loading dock. He follows the truck, bounding up the stair of the loading dock as though he belongs there.

"Excuse me," says a small Asian woman. Fenur marvels again at the locals' variations of look. The various houses come from the same stock. Their figures of speech, their dress, and their way of life differ slightly, but not as much as the melange of Las Vegas. He had heard a word for it ...a word he had perceived immediately as dangerous: monoculture. "Where are you going?" she asks.

The supply truck stops at the dock.

A few men emerge from a roll up door. Sliding it up, they take almost no notice of Fenur. "Bev, come on. You've got the clipboard," one of them says.

"Hi, yeah, I was told to meet some people here. I have a friend..." Fenur wanders off, talking over the man's complaint, his voice softening. He tries to emulate their speech patterns and feels phony. "They said to meet them on the lower levels. I didn't know how to get in." He tries to connote that someone has died. Sometimes the people here respond out of decency, but more often he finds they want to avoid an uncomfortable situation, or conflict.

"Oh. I see. Yes. You're on the right track. You should have entered on the other side." She points.

"Thank you," he says, conjuring what he hopes appears to be mournfulness he doesn't feel at Norvil's death.

Entering the hospital, the irony begins to strike him. Norvil had enjoyed the treatment he had dealt Fenur over the years. Before their arrival here, when Fenur had still been Leanor's plaything, and afterwards, when they had had their falling out. Norvil had gone to work for Stephen's hotel, but had still seen Fenur dealing, which meant the occasional side game for the hotel where as recently as their last encounter he had enjoyed wheedling and prodding at Fenur hoping that his old impassable exterior of servitude would crack. It never had. Fenur had been enjoying watching Norvil destroy himself a little at a time. His own pendant had glowed with a dull friction, at odds with the local lifestream, where as Fenur's had changed to a healthier tone. He hadn't felt healthier.

Standing in this lower hallway of the hospital, looking down at the various guidelines on the floor, color-coded to transport the user to differing wings of the hospital, he's struck by a sudden memory of Norvil in the underpeople's mountain city. All of them had gotten lost more than once. He remembers Norvil shouting at the short folk and demanding that Fenur explain his regal stature to them. He had done so with the same blank expression with which he had served the house of Nor. Angry at himself for agreeing to this, and wondering why he was unable to say no to Leanor, to simply leave with Tartus and the other two when the convention fell apart.

He reads office and laboratory nameplates.

The morgue. A man, the same one as earlier whom he talked to briefly and not as old as Fenur would have expected, suddenly emerges from the morgue doorway. Some sort of specialized doctor for the locals' dead.

A bathroom doorway to one side. Fenur turns into it, once inside walks to a stall, waits, hears the man's footsteps disappearing down the hallway. It would have been unlikely for the man from the morgue to notice him if he had tried to make himself fade there in the hallway, unlike outside where his presence was completely out of character with the surroundings (or was that type of hiding in plain sight only a different type of fading?). Fenur feels a need to be extra careful.

Fenur emerges from the bathroom and after checking the hallway, opens the door to the morgue cautiously but with enough force for it to seem as though he belongs there. An anteroom. He closes the door behind him and opens a door to the main room of the morgue.

"Excuse me?" he asks the darkened room. Empty. Through the dark, with exceptional eyes, Fenur makes out large file cabinet-style sized doors lining the walls of the room. The drawers disappear back in a double L shape away from this main area where apparently the paperwork for the bodies is processed.

Fenur looks through files on a desk. Norvil's file. Not a gun. A stabbing. Maybe with a sword? Fenur tries not to think about what the interior of the dossier says. He grimaces making a mental note to take it up with the Finn. A number in Norvil's file. On carts around the room lay three unprocessed bodies. The three bodies bear toe tags. Fenur examines each one in turn, matches the numbers in turn to the dossier. His sense of the locals' numbers is not as good as their speech and writing, strange as it seems considering how lucky he is with money, so he matches the shapes of the numbers to each exactly. He has never been able to come up with a good system of converting the economics, and always has to do it in his own tongue, in his head.

Nothing.

Looks at the numbers again and tries to figure out what the system is for putting bodies in the cases in the walls behind the file cabinet type doors. There seems to be no specific system of dates. Time ticking by as he tries to find Norvil's body... Reexamines the time of death of one of the bodies on a cart. They died before Norvil, so it stands to reason he should be on one of the carts, and the other body would be processed first. He checks the desk again, feeling that something is wrong.

Norvil's toe tag. Fenur searches the desk. The pendant of life is gone. The numbers on the toe tag match Norvil's file exactly. Norvil is gone but his toe tag remains-

The door to the antechamber, the room used for families to identify the deceased, opens.

Fenur stands in shadow and does his best to make himself fade from the lifestream. A youngish man enters the room. As he tries to shut the door, Fenur reaches out and stops it from closing, a ghost in the man's world. The man turns to his desk and sighs, flips on a desk lamp as Fenur slips through the open space in the door.

The man sits at his desk. Still willing himself towards nothingness, Fenur opens the outer door of the viewing room. The man stops digging through his files for a moment, mutters to himself and resumes. Fenur finds himself back in the hallway without engaging the man.

Down the hallway leading back towards the underground parking lot a figure – Norvil? Standing. Swaying. Tall.

Fenur trying to see but unable to focus down the length of hall. Only a scattering of lights down the hallway remain on – the late shift and money saving. The figure turns and walks into the gloom of the hospital lower level.

Fenur opens his mouth to speak and realizes it will draw attention.

He takes a few steps towards where he saw the figure, then stops. Unsure.

Deciding not to pursue, as much for the reasoning that it could be Norvil as might not be, he slips the medical file under his tshirt and follows one of the guidelines on the floor up into the public area of the hospital, acting as though he knows where he is going. No one bothers him as he follows the line on the floor.


19.

The electric cart hums through the darkened mine shaft. Tartus can barely hear it over the rest of the noise. Ahead a warning klaxon sounds as yellow earthmovers begin to back up. Diesel fumes pile upwards, grabbed by two story fans thundering in cages set into silvered tubing equally large. The exhaust system disappears back towards the surface, while a compressor runs creating positive pressure, pumping fresh air from the surface into the space. All of this gated by a solid lead airlock system. It's about four miles deep here past the main seal, the underground cranes on their tracks and the leaded compartments being swung into place.

Tartus was just up top signing paperwork for an arriving train full of the used material that is so dangerous they bury it far beneath the ground. Paperwork stamps from the Atomic Energy Commission – another one of the Washington overseers who sends him paperwork. He has never personally met anyone from one of these groups – the foreign names still trip his tongue sometimes. He has the suspicion these far away bureaucrats want to forget this place. Everything in order: papers, the train shipping containers, and they began the offload. Moving it deep into the mine.

He stops the cart and gets out. The lead foreman walks over, and a subordinate stops the giant drill he's running, looking over curiously. Big men in a small space. Tartus with the welding goggles back on his forehead, holds up a hand in the local gesture of good nature. He nods for added emphasis.

"What's up boss?" asks the foreman.

"Ronnie, you guys should move on to the west for now; it's piling up here and there's an overturned tanker on the way up on sixty-one right before the exit to the mountain. We didn't have any trouble getting around it in the LRII tonight getting in here, but it's going to be a while to clean up, and none of the removal trucks are going to be able to get up here for at least another eight hours."

The local diggers nodding.

"Anyway, if you guys move on to the west dig, we can get what you've done out of here without the rock getting so deep the 'movers are trapped."

Ronnie walks over to the man with the drill.

At the explosives lock room, high on Tom's side of the gantries at the mouth of the dig, Tartus checks the monthly sign-out sheets, as well as the room's entry and exit logs. He keys in the room's security code to its locked door and checks the logs against the explosives contained within. These logs are faxed back, usually by Tihan, to Washington D.C. Tartus, back outside the explosives lock room, signs the logs while the room's officer for this shift watches apathetically.

"How's it hanging, Tartus?" asks the local.

Tartus has no idea what this means. "Very well!" he responds jocularly and judges this correct by the man's laugh. He is counting the papers for faxing, bundling them together when his walkie-talkie chirps at him. "Hold on," he says, into the mic, finishing his sorting of the papers. "Go ahead," he says into the mic.

From the other end he hears Tihan say, "Tartus you better come back over here there's someone to see you."

"Who is it?" he asks, looking across the open space at her in the office on the wall high up on the opposing side's gantries. Connecting the two multi-storied gantries overhead, the crane track system running along the ceiling of the cavern.

"Somebody official."

"Not from the - earlier?" He corrects himself, looking at the explosive room's guard.

"Not from there."

"Tell them I'm sorting their paperwork for them, and I might as well be hip deep in mud. I'll be back when I can get there."

"They aren't from the Atomic Energy Commission." "Who are they then?" he asks.

Tihan, sounding more serious, says, "I think you just better come over here." She clicks off.

Rattled, Tartus turns back to the room's officer, signing out and taking the papers with him.

He rides the freight elevator down from Tom's side of the gantry and crosses back to his own side, riding the freight elevator on his side up to the office complex he and Tihan inhabit.

Tartus steps off the elevator onto the wall scaffolding that contains the office complex. He walks by Tihan's office where she risks a look up at him something bad.

A local in a suit sits in Tartus' office typing on one of those little devices Tartus sees everywhere. Tartus walks briskly to his desk, as the man puts the little device away. "We have a no cell phone rule here," Tartus comments.

The man nods looking up. "Mr. Tartus?" asks the man, ignoring the comment. He doesn't stand or offer to shake hands as is the custom.

"Yes, I'm Tartus. The cell phone rule is because we detonate explosives in the mines. A detonation can happen accidentally if it picks up a stray cell phone signal."

The man blanches.

"We have signs posted everywhere. I'm sure your little device works the same way as a cell phone. We use walkie-talkies because they function on a different frequency."

The man goes red, appears to be struggling not to say anything, rummages in a briefcase at the side of his chair, and pulls out a file. He opens the file. "Tartus. Last name is...?" the man leads him, looks again at the file, as he seems to recover from a fit of rage.

"I'm sorry, one of my assistants said you aren't from the AEC; who are you, if you don't mind me asking?" Tartus uses the opportunity to climb into his man-sized chair, leaving the man waiting an awkward moment, which Tartus uses in the hopes of shoving him deeper into the midden. He's dealt with many ambassadors over the time of his reign, and he's sure he understands this man's type, just from a first view. Out of the corner of his eye he sees others looking into his office at the meeting.

"I work a taskforce at the FBI." The man offers his badge across the desk, and Tartus strains to reach for it. "What was your last name again?"

"Mountain."

"Tartus Mountain. That's a very unusual name." The FBI badge says Jack Scasey. Tartus looks up, nods in a way he hopes is offhanded. "I was here yesterday but it appears you just went over to swing shift."

"We rotate every thirty days to keep everyone as fresh as possible. You work swing eventually you lose sleep. Then you can get sloppy."

"Well, it's past my bedtime." The agent seems to think this is a joke. But the sound of his voice is the tenor of steel beams being hammered together. "And I don't like helicopters. Taking one out here to Yucca at this hour, is not my idea of a good time."

"I don't follow-" Tartus stumbles as he almost says local, discerning this man's sphere of influence is larger than the desert; that it includes the surrounding mountain and coastal territories as well, quite a large landmass actually,"-politics. What exactly is it your agency does?"

"What do we do? We investigate crimes. We solve them. We protect people," Scasey intones. It sounds almost religious.

"I see." Tartus chooses his next words carefully,"This is very serious; what we do here. How may I be of assistance?"

The man stares at him, seems to be trying to look into him. Tartus waits. "We have come across several anomalous data streams here in Nevada." Tartus waits, and Scasey switches track. "Don't worry, I'm not with terror prevention." He seems to think this will set Tartus at ease, so Tartus endorses this statement with a smile and lets out a little chortle as though he understands. "No. I just work organized crime here in Vegas."

"I see." He doesn't.

"We have been following a local cards dealer who has a mafia affiliation here in town."

Fenur. Tartus raising bushy eyebrows. "I see." Wondering what the mafia is. Trying to remember the word so he can search for it online.

"We have noticed - we have this software that shows us how seemingly unrelated data streams connect. It gets used for terror prevention now. Strangely, it was developed to keep gamblers from stealing from the local casinos. Ironic, isn't it?"

As a non-native speaker, Tartus notes the misuse of the word ironic. "I don't know much about computers," Tartus tries for genial.

"Huh. So you run this whole operation, but you don't follow politics, and you don't know much about technology?" asks Scasey. "Technically, Tom over there," Tartus points to an office on the scaffolding opposite the one they are on, tiny in the distance across the great mouth of the cavern entrance,"runs the place."

"Tom Talius. Another strange name. But we couldn't find anything out of the ordinary about him at all. Pays his taxes on time. Two kids, a wife, a dog. Lives in a gated community outside the city limits." Scasey waits.

Tartus says nothing.

"You on the other hand. You haven't ever paid taxes. You live in a trailer park. You have no monetary history whatsoever. No credit cards, educational records. Nothing. We can't even figure out how you paid for the trailer. We find no birth records for you, despite what you filled in on your security app. Don't know how that one got past. None of your employment history checks out. Nothing."

Tartus waits.

"But what's more surprising is that the same is true for nearly every other person who lives in that trailer park with you," Scasey stops momentarily. "What are you? Building an army?"

Tartus laughs awkwardly. "No, I'm just a digger."

"I see," says Scasey, unimpressed. "You certainly are hard to get a hold of. Here I am at 2:10 in the AM because you're never at home."

"I'm a digger. It's the way of this life. My father was a digger. My grandfather, and his grandfather were diggers. As far back as we can remember. We have always done it this way."

"Where is your family from exactly?"

Tartus scours his brain to remember the place they had decided on, that he had put on his application. "Ohio?"

Scasey stares at him. "Coal people." Tartus agrees, relieved.

"Your accent is almost Scottish. My cousin is from Michigan, around Detroit, has this sort of marble-mouth accent, sounds almost Irish or something. Not like Minnesota at all."

Tartus says nothing. "I paid cash for the trailer," he adds thinking the statement sounds helpful.

Ignoring this, Scasey continues, "See; that's the thing: there hasn't been much coal in those veins in fifty years. Did your people move on?"

"Yes," agrees Tartus.

"Where to?"

"Wherever there was coal." He lets it hang in the air for a moment.

"At any rate," Scasey shrugging the glibness off, "We noticed that your Land..." Scasey rechecks his files, thinking there must be a mistake. "The registration for your old truck came up, and there's an intersection with this same card dealer. The one we believe is working for organized crime."

"How does that happen?" Tartus wonders allowed. He sees Tarnus wander by the office for the fifth time pretending to read files.

"We have our ways."

"I see." Tartus takes a moment, recovering his wits, by reaching behind him where he has laid his coat over a file cabinet, lifts his coat, and takes a cigar and his Zippo out of one the pockets.

"Can you wait to light that please? I'm a runner." Scasey fidgets, obviously annoyed.

"No." Tartus chews the end off the cigar and spits it in a corner.

"I'm surprised they let you smoke some place like this," Scasey tries again.

Tartus shrugs like a local. "What happens in the mine, stays in the mine."

Scasey now rattled. "How do you know this person? Another strange name; Fee Nur. Is that Finnish?"

"I don't really know Fee. Obviously. If he's associating with people like that." Tartus assumes based on the way Scasey is talking, and the little Fenur has told him that they are in fact "people like that".

Scasey makes a grunting sound. He takes out a pen and writes something in the margin of the file he's holding.

"Don't really know him? That's not the same as don't know him." "Right," Tartus confirms.

"So how do you know him?" Scasey asks.

"Our families have a relationship," Tartus offers.

Scasey takes a moment to recover, going through various fast blanches from which Tartus infers he finds this statement dubious. Just like an incompetent ambassador. "At any rate..." he says, rising and grabbing his briefcase, then putting the file away,"You will probably be hearing from me again. In the meantime take my card, if you see Fee Nur, tell him I would like to talk to him. It's important." Scasey hands over a small calling card Tartus palms, teeth chewing the cigar. He doesn't stand.

"I'll show myself out," says Scasey making his way to the door.

Tihan in the next office looks through the glass divider at Tartus. Tartus ignoring her: Not now.

20.

The LRII putters down the gravel embankment into the mobile home parking area, windshield suddenly brilliant with morning light. After the swingshift they are tired, the sun affecting them, as it would at home, though their internal clocks always seem slightly confused by the differences in the lengths of days between home and here. Other oddities like adjusting to weighing slightly less, the direction water swirls in drains, and the stars always offering novelty and confusion.

Tarnus turns the LRII off. It dies with a series of histrionic metal squeaks and a flatulent sigh of released air.

Hano waits in front of Tartus' Airstream. The three exchange glances.

"Find Morno," Tartus instructs. Tihan climbs out, following his directions.

"I need her," Hano barks at Tartus, from his place leaning against an old Japanese roadster.

Tihan runs down to Morno's trailer and pounds on the door. A squeaky screen door opens and they hear a quarrelsome exchange, followed by Morno returning to the interior of his trailer while the screen door bangs shut.

Continuing over this, Tartus says,"Good to see you too." He has the welding goggles pulled down over his eyes in the morning light. He adds soberly,"No one is keeping her." "I can make my own decisions," Tihan interrupts, returning. Tartus, are you sure you don't need me here?" she asks without missing a beat, in order to give him the opportunity of retaining some modicum of kingly privilege.

Tartus gives up, as she needles him. "I'm not even sure what I can do right now. What is it, Hano?"

"Much is changing between their world and our world. Something is happening. Is he coming?" asks Hano, referring to Morno.

"No," Tihan says.

"There are certain things I cannot accomplish without another. I need the only one even remotely qualified," Hano looks grim.

"Tartus, I can stay-"

Tartus waves Tihan off. "Take Tihan, and do what you can then. "What have your experiments shown?"

"Fluxuations. I cannot say where yet. I need to return to the crossing point, and make readings. You said you felt it at the mine?"

"It felt the same as the crossing point," Tihan says.

"It felt like the accumulation," Tarnus adds.

"It would be a lucky thing for the point to be moving so linearly across this landscape," Hano says. "Morno came to see me – he implied he acquired the dark mead at Fenur's hotel."

"Morno has it?" Tarnus exclaims. "We had been wondering what had happened to it."

"Let me speak with him about it," Hano says, marching to Morno's Airstream.

As he wanders down the row of trailers, Tartus worried, remarks,"How did he find you?" to Hano's back.

Hano bangs on the door with a fist until Morno opens the door. Hano punches Morno. Morno doubles up holding his eye. "GIVE ME THE DARK MEAD!" Hano shouts.

"Alright, alright..." Morno says, giving up.

Hano barges past him, Morno letting him through without further argument, waving for Tihan to help him out.

"Not very kingly – if he was looking to start a new line of the mountain clan," Tihan observes.

"At least Morno's version of subterfuge has yet to be dangerous," Tarnus responding.

"Except for the accumulation."

"There is that."

A few minutes later the two have the dangerous cargo loaded in the rear hatch of the Japanese roadster.

Tihan and Hano get in the old Japanese car. It starts in a gout of white smoke and putters out of the trailer park.

"Go get Morno, would you?" Tartus says to Tarnus. He walks into his trailer.

Inside the Airstream under the fold down couch Tartus sleeps on, he finds wooden box long lost and dusts it off. He takes the implements of his rule out

He had forgotten to wear his signet ring at the gathering. Annoyed at himself. How could he have forgotten? A royal stamp follows. Royal colored wax in stick form for imprinting. The color the same as his signet; a color by law only he could use. He takes a ballpoint and a sheet of notebook paper and writes in a sharp script of his own people:

Problems with the locals, Queen of the House of Nor. Will your Majesty accept my apologies and grant me leave while I deal with my own subjects? May we rejoin you late today? Please do not punish young Fenur for my overscheduling, as I fully intend to continue my defense of him, as far as is necessary, for this matter concerns him as well. I will explain fully as soon as I am able.
    Tartus,
    Last King-

He grabs a new piece of paper and starts over, finishing:

Tartus,
    Remaining King of the Underpeople

He frowns at the phrasing, then folds the note three times.
    "My Lordship?" says Morno formally, arriving at Tartus' door, his left eye darkening. Tarnus flanks him. Both look like they have been in a minor fight.
    "One moment, Morno," Tartus says sealing the note with royal wax. He melts the wax using the Zippo. He seals the letter by pressing the wax with his signet ring and then starts to take the ring off his finger. Stops, thinking better of it, and rises. "Take this to the queen of Nor. Do not let any of her subordinates try and force their will upon you. Deliver it only to her. Use this royal stamp as admission, and also your long time companionship with the houses. Go now." Morno tries to take the letter, and Tartus pulls it back a

moment, Morno with a hand still on it. "We will speak about the mead later," Tartus warns.

"Yes, your Lordship." Morno takes the note and disappears into the morning light. The sound of Morno's motorcycle starting up, then disappearing.

Tartus says,"After so many problems with his clan, my clan, even here, I am surprised when things... ...become difficult... We will rely on him, and force him to become reliable." Tarnus agrees brusquely.

Tarnus repeats an old saying,"Reliable in the mine, or alone outside." Then looking for Tartus's consent,"I should do as Hano suggested and search his residence."

Tartus agrees, giving him the command to do it.

In a few minutes Tarnus returns. "Nothing."

"Then where did the mead come from? Who could have kept such a large crate of it?"

"Perhaps one person each kept a bottle. The crate could have been broken down and hidden amongst our other items in the crossing."

Tartus considers, says to Tarnus,"Gather everyone else. We must proceed to the houses' gathering together as one people of separate clans, rather than in our more anarchic natural state. If the locals are aware of us, then our time here-"

"Police!" yells someone from across the park."Tartus..."

Tarnus starts.

"I know." Tartus grabs a rucksack from a stowage bin he has kept stashed for an emergency like this.

Tarnus lunges back inside his own trailer and reappears with a rucksack of his own stuffed to the brim.

Tartus turns back at the door, remembering the royal chest he has left out; closing it, he pushes it into his sack. Police cars charge through the mobile home park throwing up dust, tires rumbling and spewing gravel. The cars swerve blocking exits as the diggers try to flee, as they come out onto makeshift stoops in boxer shorts to see what is happening, and return to interiors to make off with what they can scrounge in the chaos.

"I suppose I should have been more accommodating this morning with the locals," Tartus offers.

"It wouldn't have made any difference," Tarnus says fatalistically.

Cops out of the passenger side doors of cruisers tackle people, throwing them to the ground, tripping runners with nightsticks, handcuffing others who still struggle. Slow to start, some of the diggers succeed in escaping past the line of police cruisers, others are wrestled out of vehicles with keys pulled from ignitions by uniforms. Still others are hemmed in before they get out of the parking lot. Others rumble off the well-worn parking area and out into the desert making for access roads and deer trails, followed by black and white trucks. Sirens wail across the hardened sand. All trying to divert the locals from Tartus and his subordinate. A few police stay behind to help with the round up. Two heavily barred police vans are loaded with those captured.

Tarnus watching the unfolding disaster. "They weren't supposed to be able to remember us..."

Three police running towards them, holster snaps undone, hands on pistol grips.

"Tarnus, with me!" shouts Tartus, behind the wheel of the LRII again.

The LRII springs forward past the Airstream and off-road, heading the opposite direction from the other escapees.

A few cruisers try and follow them down a short but sharp ravine, one makes it onto the hard dry riverbed near the trailer park, but winds up wallowing in deeper unpacked sand eating an oversized cactus when the LRII turns into the desert from the river bed.

A tall climb to an access road while the riveted aluminum body of the LRII creaks and groans. Tarnus reaches, nearly straining out of his seat for the upper rib of the truck. He tries to use it to push himself back down firmly. At slightly too short, he either has to reach so far he's no longer in contact with the seat, or risk falling out of the doorless shell, seatbelts long since having rotted away. Tartus laughs maniacally from the driver's seat as they scramble up the hill.

"What about the police?" he asks as they crest the ridge.

"Long gone," Tarnus says looking over his shoulder.

"Good thing we mapped out escapes." They turn onto an access road.

"We should have Tihan with us."

"She'll be fine with Hano."

"I hope so," Tarnus says peering over the sill at the blacktop blurring away behind them.

Tartus leaves the LRII running in the already baking parking lot of a rundown minimart, and walks to a set of pay phones. Not many left many of these pay phones left, but out here in the desert cell coverage is so spotty a portable would be useless. Anyway, a local contrivance would put them more at risk... Tartus shakes the thought off; it's already too late.

Standing in the shade he rummages in his dusty trenchcoat and finds the card Jack Scasey gave him. He looks in his pockets again for change, finds none, and says to Tarnus,"You have any change?"

Tarnus just looks at him, pushes out of the LRII, looks under the seat from his new position on the gooey tarmac, finds nickels, dimes, a quarter or two and marches them over to Tartus.

Tartus picks up the handset and notices it's covered in crusted vomit just before putting it to his ear. He recoils and drops it, leaving it swinging by its cord. He walks to a second phone and picks it up. Tarnus stands back out of the sun.

Tartus waits while the phone rings. It rings through to Scasey's voicemail.

Tartus hangs up, irritated, not leaving a message. "Voicemail," he explains to Tarnus.

Tarnus says,"What do you think Hano wants with Tihan?" Tartus starts to answer when the phone he was just on rings.

The two exchange a look, and Tartus picks it up, saying nothing.

"This is Scasey."

"This is Tartus." "You called me," Scasey says. Not a question.

"Yes," Tartus waits. When nothing is forthcoming he asks,"How did you call me back here?"

"Just making sure the line is clean." Scasey hangs on the phone, still waiting.

"You told me you weren't interested in... us."

"When you see Fee Nur, why don't you ask him about Luigi Vertosi. And about that Japanese hitman he knows. You want to be left alone? Some information would be a start. You could ask him where he got all his money - or do you already know?" Scasey is sliding over into what seems to Tartus nearly another accent. Scasey seems angry, and this slippage gives him away. The man seems tired as well, probably from finding them on the swing shift. "What sort of familial relationship is it you have exactly? Maybe I've been looking at this wrong. The mafia with access to what's up in the mountain is a scary thought."

Tartus frowns, and makes a decision, and says bluntly,"I don't know what the mafia is. Apparently, it's some sort of crime organization. So deal with them. Back home, we would just bury them alive. No more problem. What does this have to do with my people? Why did you call the police to raze us this morning?"

"You knew what could happen."

"You specifically told me you weren't interested in me or-" he stops at my people, registers he just said it and should not repeat it, instead says,"my home."

"Like I said, information makes it easier to overlook your little enclave. You don't like the government? Fine; we can leave you alone. But you have friends. And your friends interest us."

"Fee Nur," Tartus uses the man's pronunciation,"I've known him a long time. He's unlucky. That's all."

"This morning you barely knew him-"

"I do barely know him!" Tartus unable to follow phone protocol.

Scasey just talks over him. "-If he's so unlucky where's all that money coming from? You know how long he's been living out there by the airport?"

"You know what I mean. You should leave him alone."

"Like I said, he's just a stepping stone to Vertosi."

"So you destroy my life? You told me you had no interest in our diggers' camp. You just arrested half of them!"

"That was the local PD. We simply alerted them to the situation; none of you have ID's, social security numbers, you name it. If local officials want to know who's living in their town, they should be able to find that out. Don't you think that's fair? Do you even have a driver's license? You want to be left alone, you know what you have to do. Then maybe I can help with the charges on the miners."

Tartus has no idea what the man wants him to do. He holds Scasey's business card up and examines the man's name. "You have made an enemy today, Jack Scasey."

"That's Federal Agent Scasey, Mr. Mountain. Do you know what you're doing? Are you threatening a federal agent?" Scasey trying for menacing. Tartus finds it buffoonish.

"I hope that we meet again," Tartus says, and hangs up.

Tarnus watches Tartus circumspectly, trying to keep his opinion to himself.

"Come on; we have to get to Leanor for the gathering," Tartus gruffly ignores him, stalking back towards the LRII.

As they pull out of the minimart, Tarnus asks,"You think we can get Hano to show up? Maybe we can resolve who smuggled the mead across?"

"No."


21.


The old Japanese car parallel parks on the street at Hano's junkstore.

"You never wash your car," Tihan says. A statement, not a criticism.

"No. I never wash it. Thus it is safe to keep on the street."

As they get out, Tihan says,"I never thought we would be here this long. To learn these little customs."

"I never thought we would make it through," Hano grabs a bag he always keeps with him out of the back seat, slams the rusty door and continues on into the store without looking back. Tihan follows, also anxious to get out of the sun.

"How am I going to be able to help, Hano? I never even began training. Inside the shop seems slightly cleaner than it did previously. Or maybe it's just more orderly.

"If they had listened to me and allowed you to train... If they had accepted you as the person you are, liking who and what you like..." he stops. "Ah, well too late. We will make do. Natural understanding of the stones' inherent spirit is most of it. You have that already. With the unusual make up of the mines here – well, maybe training would not have benefited you for this place." Tihan sit in a green oversized chair the stuffing is falling out of, hands on armrests, wood burnished smooth by years of use examining the scabrous settlings of epochs of a technological society.

She examines a reflecting telescope with noticeably less dust.

"You're using this," she says.

"Trying to find home out there..." Hano says, dropping his bag of wares,"I must try and reopen the pass."

"I thought it was closed forever. That it has to open from a new locale here to somewhere else at home now?" Tihan trying not to sound surprised.

"So we thought. Or maybe not to home – maybe to somewhere completely different again. Perhaps. In which case we are safe from the accumulation. Unless what they are becomes more conscious – disagree with the ones who say they have a will of their own. We shall see.

"Tartus said that you could feel them right at the end point of the dig?" Hano probing.

"Yes. The dig has continued on a few yards now, but that spot still feels... I don't know. Hot."

"A new hot spot but close to the original. Hmm..." Hano pulls his beard, thinking. "We have a connection to both of these places."

Tihan waits, just listening.

"Have you wondered how our accents in the language of the locals came out as something recognizable to them as a specific place? Same for the houses." He considers, says aloud,"All places are connected."

Tihan thinks, then says,"Are you saying the other places we can feel are closer than the mages thought? I have wondered why we were led to somewhere where we could still pass as diggers. It is difficult to imagine a place that wouldn't have something like what we do, but..."

"Perhaps this place was easier to access for us. The song of stone woven for the opening; well, we called for help from the rock we come from. Perhaps it answered," Hano stops. His mood seems to alter as he says,"We are slipping into their - the locals' - ways.

Would they slip into ours if we led them across?"

Tihan considers. "I wonder. Or would they age differently, as I can see us aging differently here."

"Maybe this is the way it is because we are part of it. If we exit, will it change into something different because of our absence? Would our home be changed by one of these people crossing over?" Hano frowns.

"It is very dangerous to open it where it is, especially if the accumulation is right there. And we don't know if it will leads us back to the Pass of Heaven. It could be the accumulation has found another crossing which happens to emerge near our first. And if it does, we would then have to return to the battle right then. Maybe in a place we are unfamiliar with. And there is no retreat from the pass. We must recheck the door that led us through."

Hano broods momentarily then lets out a rattling sigh. "You must do as I ask, Tihan. Regardless of how it may appear, I am trying to help our people. Better to die there, as who we were meant to be, than be subsumed here."

"I had not thought of it. It really is just another kind of accumulation we are beset with here, if we slip away into their lifestream."

Hano coming to a decision. "We cannot let that happen. We may have to return to the Pass of Heaven."


22.


Introductions and formalities conducted by Konor at this second parley in the hotel conference room. Vilhan continuing where Konor leaves off. Vilhan taking up his more traditional place and role behind Leanor,"The lesser ones found their end. And we should consider Fenur's request, your request as a request in their absence? Your defense is absurd."

"You are absurd." Fenur rejoins. "You know not what happened to the people of the Far Sea at the pass. None of us do. You should have acted."

Vilhan counters,"You dare to suggest the greater houses are incompetent?"

"I suggest that you are incompetent. A marriage of convenience does not make you King," Fenur returns haughtily.

"Fenur!" shouts Leanor.

Vilhan continuing through Leanor's outburst: "-So says the slave."

"Vilhan this breach will not stand," rumbles Tartus. "Do not suggest that those unable to defend themselves are lesser than you again. Or that the underpeople have done less than their utmost for the houses."

Leanor risks a quick warning glance behind her at Vilhan.

Vilhan ignores Leanor, persisting on his line of attack,"How long have we waited for the last mage to find a return? And you arrive late, with no news, and impugn us in this way?"

Leanor trying to regain control with hand gestures while the others talk.

"I am but a slave," returns Fenur. "Other than save the greater houses, what have I done? What have you done?" he asks Vilhan. "You are a coward, a fool and a dandy. Nothing more than a laughingstock." Fenur turns,"Leanor?"

Vilhan spits on Fenur from the dais. "That is what I think of you and your house, slave."

Fenur recoils as Tartus draws his axe, and puts a foot on the stage.

"WE WAITED LONG ENOUGH ON YOUR PRESENCE!" Leanor shouting, in full panic. "Have them removed."

As he advances on Vilhan with the axe, Tartus says,"My apologies. Please, Leanor, allow my defense to continue," Tartus trying to shove through the advancing guards towards Vilhan. The guards take the axe before he can swing it.

"Have them removed," Leanor commands again from slightly outside the fray.

"Queen, they drew weapons and advanced on you and the King.

There must be blood." Tartus struggling. Fenur gone limp. "Have them removed," Leanor repeats looking Tartus in the eye.

Something about her has always been able to do this to him. The convention room's attention welded to the confrontation. The guards pulling Tartus and Fenur away, disarmed.

"You have counseled us wrongly in so many things," she says.

"We took you in!" Tartus exclaims, furious at being physically propelled out of the room by the guards.

Fenur shouts,"Counseled? If you hadn't needed so much counseling - if it weren't for your indecisiveness none of them would have-"

"REMOVE THEM!" Leanor roars. Konor, and a few others of the houses' formal detail bodily grab the two, dragging them towards the door of the hall.

"You are no queen!" Fenur hurls across the hall as Konor shoves him towards the door. "After what I have done for the houses-"

"And you could not complete the simplest of tasks I have set for you!" she rejoins. "You, last of your house, make demands of me?"

"The pendant was gone! I am last BECAUSE OF YOU! If Norton were king, or if you had any sense to lead, you would not-" Leanor's detail throws the two to the ground in the lobby. Fenur shouts as they close the doors,"Norvil wanders alone! He tries to find his rest!"

"Like all the others you are responsible for," she says from the hotel convention room dais, as the door closes on them.

Tarnus puts his hands on Fenur's chest, coming up to the two from his place where he has been waiting in the lobby. "Not now." The two stare at the closed doors past him. Tourists wander by risking glances at the group thrown from the convention room. They look at the sign and the doors to the room: WELCOME: "PEOPLE FROM ANOTHER WORLD!" Back at the group. Echoes of the shouting having died away. Some of the tourists smirk.

"Tartus?" Tarnus asks.

Tartus seems to be jerked from his berserker's fog by this. "Yes. We will wait." He turns on his heel and the other two follow him.

Behind them they hear,"Wait."

Norton standing in the lobby, the door closing behind him. The three stop. Norton walks across the lobby to them. "I will see what I can do." "What was said..." Fenur begins.

"The enslavement of the people of the Far Sea was a terrible error in judgment by the those of my generation. Among the eldest there is not even a word for your people. We did not believe you could be the same... as us, yet..." Norton struggles for politic words and fails,"Yet so different."

Tartus says,"Forgive my outburst."

"There is nothing to forgive. It is true. Without the underpeople, the houses would no longer exist. In trying to end the slave trade of the people of the Far Sea, Morno and I thought we could unite the houses and clans under one banner; freedom for all. We were wrong. I must apologize for my people."

Tartus makes clear that he doesn't accept this by his body language. "You can not apologize for an entire people. Only do what you can. That is all we ask."

Norton unshaken. "She is..." He takes a deep breath. Leaves the rest unsaid.

Tartus nearly agape. Tarnus stunned. Fenur near boiling.

"All this time-" Fenur starts.

Tarnus taps the two of them lightly: Konor at the door to the convention room.

Norton looks at Fenur for a moment, unreadable. Stalks back past Konor into the convention room.

The three continue out.

"One moment," Fenur stands, hands on the roof of the car, pressing into the scorching metal in the maze-like parking lot.

The two wait.

"He did all of this - and never - he still couldn't - he was nearly king!"

"Being king is as much about what needs to be done, as what one would like to do," Tartus says. Tarnus purses lips inside of deep mustache and beard.

"My life was wasted."

"Only you can decide that." Tarnus asks,"Isn't that the meaning of the pendants?" "What?" asks Fenur.

"The pendants rot and fall when the life of the wearer becomes meaningless. Then the member of the house, the wearer, fades."

"Fades and wanders south," Fenur intones, citing something the two diggers are unfamiliar with. "My kind never wore pendants. Until..." "Do you still love her?" Tarnus asks.

Fenur looks at him. Grimaces. "I have to go." The door thumps shut solidly, and the V6 springs to life.

23.

The wind blows out of the east, a Santa Ana. Gray clouds fill the sky to brimming. First drops, fat, pull dust from the air, mix with oil pushed out of cement by the humidity, create the smell of a coming storm. Fenur still fuming after returning to his suite, changing clothes and showering, and then calling the Finn. By the time he got off the highway he was collected enough to continue.

Luigi Vertosi at the door of the house. A suburb of Las Vegas. Fenur had nearly gotten lost. All the houses are nearly alike, separated by landscaping and ornamentation, different doors, insets of windows. Money whispering in virtually identical color schemes. Some he throws cards to call them McMansions and gripe about the power Vegas sucks from the grid. He laughs dutifully not sure exactly what this means.

His pendant throbs dully against his neck as the vintage sports car pulls to the curb, waved in by Vertosi in a set of flip-flops, summer weight raw silk pants, a short sleeve dress shirt that looks like it was cut whole for him. He's holding a cup of coffee and the New York Times under an arm where it rubs ink on his shirt. Nearby the Finn looking on.

"Pull to the curb," Vertosi shouts through the glass, waving him over. "My cousins are showing up later I want them to have somewhere to park; they're bringing all the kids and I don't want them to have to unload in the street."

"Hello, Mr. Vertosi," Fenur says.

"Hey, kid. How's it going?" LV laughs.

"Lou, you're going to get wet!" shouts the Finn from up the driveway heading toward him across the lawn with a golf umbrella.

"Ah! What do you know? I wanna look at the car. Rev it once for me," Vertosi says to Fenur, putting his hands against the door, the window still up. The old man looks back at the mid-engine space behind the seats. Fenur hits the accelerator and the V6 roars. Vetosi laughs. "Enzo..." he shakes his head. "They do sound nice. Come on."

"Lou you're getting your shirt... Why don't you just get a news agent on the net like everyone else?" the Finn taking the paper for the old man, watching his feet on the now slippery grass and standing back with an arm outstretched sheltering him under the large multicolored umbrella.

"I don't trust the internet, you know that Finn. What am I? Ninety year old? Don't tell me what to do. Anyway, I have somebody to wash my shirts." He turns to Fenur,"How do you survive in there with the windows rolled up and no air conditioning?"

Fenur seems surprised,"I never really notice. Or rarely anyway."

"You're a weird kid."

Inside the house isn't exactly what Fenur was expecting. It's spare, full of paintings which are abstract fields of color, towering plants and bent wood furniture with simple lines. It doesn't fit the house. The room he is led to look onto a side yard with a terraced herb garden with fresh water running through peat to aerate it, a waterfall at the top pounds stones, throwing mist into the air to keep the herbs wet. "My wife's herb garden. We imported the olive trees from Calabria so there would be enough shade. The damn water costs me a fortune in the dry. Have a seat."

"But today it's raining." The herbs foreign and exotic to Fenur, the piercing smells like colors popping in his head. "Yeah, thank God for small favors." Vertosi laughs again seeming genuinely pleased to see Fenur.

Fenur eyes the Finn, who isn't in a talkative mood. The Finn stares out the window.

"Good job, by the way on that thing," Vertosi offers.

Fenur nods but says nothing, knowing this is the most appropriate response.

"You and Sato. You both proved reliable - but you don't seem to like each other much. Right?" Fenur moves his head side to side in a gesture of not caring. Vertosi continues,"I don't like to pair guys who don't get along. It leads to problems eventually. It's just one of those things. You two going to have a problem? A thing goes well, I like to keep things the way they are. He doesn't talk. I understand that irks some guys."

"I'm ok with it."

"If you aren't ok, you say, understand, Fee?" the Finn offers turning from the window. "It's more important that business go smoothly, than anyone set of people makes money. Got it?"

"I understand."

Luigi Vertosi looks at him, gauging,"You really don't care do you?"

"No, mister Vertosi."

"Call me Lou." "Alright." Fenur decides he will continue with Mr. Vertosi. "Ok. We got other things. Finn will fill you in. We got a guy in the field office here works RICO. We have a real problem with someone in that office. But like I said, that part's for the Finn here. How's it going with you?"

"I'm ok."

"Yeah? You need anything? Everything going smoothly over at your work?"

"As far as I know, everything is fine." "And the hotel? Because your friend got... didn't he?"

"Norvil wasn't my friend."

"You have anything to do with that; working off the books?"

"I don't know what happened to Norvil. I'm not sure anyone does."

"We didn't do it. I'm telling you that straight out," the old man says looking into Fenur's eyes.

"Ok." Fenur feeling something from somewhere, he can't define, doesn't know where it's coming from. Rain now pattering at the back windows here in this little meeting room.

"I know Norvil was in that hotel, with the last thing. I know you were in the car. But it wasn't us. It was around the same time, but you have to believe that it wasn't us. You understand what I'm saying?" asks Vertosi.

"I do."

"You believe me?"

Fenur takes an appropriate amount of time, and nods his head.

"I do, Mr. Vertosi."

"Ok, kid. You gonna stay for food?" The Finn makes a barely perceptible headshake.

"I can't, Mr. Vertosi, I'm sorry."

"Ok. The Finn will give you the details." He slaps Fenur's upper arm one last time.

On the back patio, at the base of Luigi Vertosi's wife's herb garden, the two take cover under an olive tree to avoid the rain and get wet anyway from the small artificial waterfall splashing down to rocks. Carp in small terraced pools winding though the tiers of herbs. Fenur looks back into the house.

"His name's Scasey." Fenur looks up at mention of the name from Leanor's office. "He needs to understand this is a business like any other business. We'll come up with something for you and Sato eventually."

Fenur nods watching fat drops of rain hit the water, shining little jewels off the locals' strange plants for spicing. "Alright, I'll do it. But I'll need something to protect myself. A sword." "A sword?" the Finn starts laughing.

"I was a fencing champion."

"You were a fencing champion." The Finn laughing so hard at the unexpected request, and the weirdness of a card dealer/fencing champion, his eyes are tearing up.

Fenur frowns. "I can't obtain what I need here." The Finn trying not to double over, puts his arms around his girth. "Well, I hear katanas are the best swords humans have ever made," offers the Finn. "Although I'd pay good money to see you walking down Fremont Street dragging a Claymore after you." "What?" Fenur puzzling.

"Giant Scottish sword," the Finn offers. "I was president of my D&D club at my frat – did you know that?"

"No."

"Some people are surprised. They don't think a guy like me went to college." The Finn waits, expecting a challenge – it almost seems like a strange sort of baiting or character assessment the Finn is acting out. "I have a Ph.d. in Linguistics - I studied okie speech patterns in migrations from Ireland all the way through the Appalachians and out to California." The Finn relaxes when Fenur proffers no ridiculing of the big man. Fenur waits until the Finn continues. "Okay... you know, whatever you're talking about; I believe you. Finish the job, we'll find one. The yaks have to have one laying around somewhere. You can have whatever kind of sword you want. You sure you wouldn't rather have a nice clean gun?" asks the Finn.

"Has to be a sword," says Fenur.

24.

A short dreary drive through the facelessness of suburbia.

Townhouses jammed up against each other sharing common walls, little window portals peaking out at communal areas, little touches making the prefab personal. It reminds him of the cliffs of Wind's Breath somehow, especially in the baked earth colors the designers chose. An econobox parked in front of one of the houses.

Sato out of the car, pulling his bag after him. He motions for the slip of paper Fenur holds. Looks at the numbers. Fenur and Sato concur - same numbers as the license of the econobox. Nods to Sato who unzips the bag on the front seat, saying things in Japanese to himself: a ski mask, kubotan - a kind of non-lethal nightstick - a small serrated knife he pockets, and a tiny pistol also disappearing inside the jacket of his suit. Both of them already wearing thin deerskin gloves. "In case," he manages in English.

Sato gestures to him. Fenur gives him the note from the Finn.

"You're supposed to hold it up and say 'Read,'" Fenur instructs. Sato holds the note up to Fenur and says,"Ryid."

"Read."

"Ryed." Fenur accedes this may be good enough.

As this is transpiring, Scasey's family emerges from one of the many doorways that almost seem clones of each other and head towards a small crossover vehicle.

Sato opens the door and begins walking towards them.

25.

Arid wind and LR. Tarmac unpeeling. Tartus mesmerized by the drive thinking on the current circumstances.

A few have days pass. They hear nothing more of the convention. A few diggers drift back to camp. Others call Tartus' voicemail at the mine. Tartus checking his voicemail from payphones. Most say minor outstanding warrants have not been resolved, or just report harassment. But some say they have had visits from officials with badges, agencies they aren't aware of, and have been questioned. Pressure is being put on them for everything from minor offenses to things that are slightly more serious: they owe money on traffic tickets, minor brawling incidents, or they never showed to court appointments for taxes and bounced checks. The things that would have eventually evaporated in their life here before, as their and the locals' two separate planes receded from a moment's interaction. This is how it has been since they arrived.

Until now.

When those that were apprehended call, they don't realize these same officials are probably monitoring Tartus' work phone. They speak in the language of the underpeople, but Tartus wonders if the locals will think it's a code, and how long it will take them to decipher it.

The scrub and sun glint its own kind of portentousness.

Trying to break the silence, Tarnus muses,"They are having pro wrestling on the strip."

Tartus says nothing, not wanting to talk, and unable to come up with a solution to their problems. Tarnus aware that he will turn things over and over unless interrupted. Also aware it sometimes ends in axe throwing.

Tarnus waits on an answer.

"Wrestling..." Tartus barely paying attention. Finally, "What is the difference between professional wrestling and wrestling for sport?"

"It is on television?" offers Tarnus, not having seen wrestling for pure sport.

"You know I do not watch much television." Tartus trying to forestall further conversation.

"You enjoy those shows about the workings of the undercities here - and archeology. Also the programs about building large contraptions or the ones about how some things are only myths while others which are supposedly myths, are true. And the ones about the human diggers."

"Yes." Tartus affirms against his will.

Tarnus continues, "In some ways the stories of wrestling are the same or better than the hero stories of home. With television you can see it happen; that's inherently better than the songs and the plays of home." Tarnus continues staring out the side of the LRII, not perceiving the change in Tartus, "We are like the stories of the old heroes. Or even those of wrestling."

Tartus stirred, rumbling, "How so?"

"It is a performance where we play our parts. The old heroes weren't one kind of thing despite how they are portrayed in the songs and plays. Same with wrestling. You act as king. Leanor as queen. While we wait on the sidelines. Tenur is the unknown - the one who upsets the story, draws us into what plays out."

"That is always a bad person. I do not believe he is a bad person. This is not dress up for children - it is not a narrative. It is life. Our livelihood-"

"You know that even the likes of Tihan have never cared for the dig itself. It is a living but not the thing which sustains for many of us. Livelihoods are sustenance as well as income and history, and tradition. Many care not even for the stories of it. Or even for the lodes."

"Tihan loves the metals as much as any one of us."

"Yes. But she doesn't care for it. Not like she did for becoming one of the mages."

"Perhaps not," Tartus concedes. "This is different from Fenur he has made a way for himself here – it makes a kind of sense. Look at what was lost of his peoples - airships, and ice vessels, steam technology unknown to us. As well as their own secret ways. All the things of the Far Sea peoples." Tartus thinks a moment, considering all that has happened, and wondering what the future might be comprised of. "We must rescue those arrested. I worry it could be repeated among us here." Tartus adds,"What happened." Clarifying that he means the fate of the Far Sea peoples at the Pass of Heaven and what of theirs' was lost.

"I am your direct subordinate and chief advisor. I have no ambition of my own for power. How long have I worked in this capacity for you? If you continue along this line, trying to rescue those who ran afoul of the local powers, it is my duty to advise you that you may expose us," Tarnus cautions redoubtably.

"And what shall we do? Leave them to rot in this foreign land?" Tartus shouts at him, finally cracking.

An argument over how to proceed to retrieve their people. They have been driving around for hours with no where to go, trying to decide. The shouting becomes so intense Tartus pulls over to the side of the highway. It's not like the good-natured fisticuffs of most of their adventuring. Gravel flies and brake squeal. Tarnus springs down from the LRII, Tartus around the side out of roaring traffic. Straining voices over it. Suddenly the argument has turned to the previous topic.

"What were you expecting her to say?" Tarnus returns.

"I..."

"You were the king-" "I am the only king left to us!" Tartus shouts. "Then how would you have been different in the old country?" Tarnus asks. "We are all changing. You are not immune."

Tartus disagreeing. "Lives are... It is different here. No one is expendable now!"

"You dare to lecture us on calling you Tar, or drinking the swill the local call beer. Or on how loud we raise our voices in a foreign land? And when counsel caution you play the magnanimous king. I counsel us on trying to fit in and make our way and you correct me that we lose ourselves here. But when.

You used... How would you have responded to an outrage like this from the houses in the past?"

"Our egos - my ego - does not get to enter into it; except when we speak of remembering who is king. Not why. You shame us all by calling me by a shortened name not my own. By calling me 'man' – it would have been AN INSULT in the old country on par with likening me to a tree – if these ...whatever they are; weak, insolent, lazy, backward... ...people existed on our side. You would not have lived for the insult. But I do not get to decide who is king or queen among the houses. Or how competent they are."

"You do it out of guilt for Fenur." Tarnus bitter.

"Nothing could have prevented what happened to him. But yes – we OWE."

"They owe. WE do not." Tarnus asks,"Remember what you said to me at the pass? You did not believe in destiny."

"Maybe..." Tartus turns away.

"You have changed your mind. Or made the decision that day not to believe in it. The convenience of being king. Was saying 'there is no destiny' intended for him? Because you could not stomach more war? War with the houses even as we were surrounded by the accumulation? Did you say it so that he would be able to do what he did? You preferred to try and make him one of us when our demand was that the Far Sea people be freed. But he was not one of us. You preferred not to make an issue of the near civil war when they agreed and the Far Sea peoples' anger was loosed. And now you prefer to ignore what Fenur has become. Which is it? Does it matter what he does? Can the houses punish him if he is the one who has best adjusted? Can we blame him? Can you blame Tihan and myself for trying to find a way here, Tar? And then; why didn't you say something when Leanor challenged you, king?"

Tartus stands mute for a moment. Weakly he says,"If the locals are remembering us, now is the time to try and unite - to overlook these petty arguments from the past. We must try-"

"You are so careful, and yet so rash, the clans are broken!" Tarnus turns and walks away from the LRII at the side of the road leaving Tartus to explain to the sand and scrub brush.

26.

Eventually Tartus has to return to work.

Tartus sleeps under the LRII in the desert, in a deep cleft of rock in the shade with the welding goggles covering his eyes. It is nearly impossible for him to sleep outside, with his nature. He trades shifts with the other supervising locals so he misses Tarnus when he shows up and doesn't have to become a complete day sleeper. Hears of Tarnus trading shifts as well. The nights he spends looking up at an alien sky and trying to figure out what the local mythology is. An aftermarket 12 volt DC outlet in the LRII allows him to make dinners on his hotplate from his office.

Tarnus holed up in a Travelodge near the airport, where the deep rumble of planes disrupts his sleep, but pleasantly, something of the thundering of deep digging in it. Tarnus has been distant and slightly angry, feeling the second day of the convention could have been something other than the debacle it was. He checks his work messages from an airport payphone; one of the few payphones left. If the locals didn't know about Fenur, he could have used his phone to warn him. The weight of this interloper Scasey heavier on the king's second than on Tartus himself. It seems to be always the way. It leaves Tarnus wondering: Warn the houses? But still with the locals monitoring the incomings and outgoings, it would have just put them in danger.

No one hears from Tihan or Hano.

Morno already returned to the mine, having left before the camp was overrun to deliver Tartus' message to the convention. He returned to find the camp decimated.

Morno checks files and the vast cubbyhole system of notifications for the miners, also making notations about how many they have lost. He tosses a file of his work to Tartus when he sees him punching in outside the locker room and shower system contained in a series of double-wides at the mouth of the mine. They are still digging through rock to install permanent changing rooms for each sex. Tihan's suggestion - she hears the local females talking; they're fewer than the men, but Tartus concedes their point, despite his aversion to acknowledging sexual differentiation outside of courtship. Strangely, the original plans didn't call for it.

"Tom wants to see you," Morno mumbles.

"Good work," Tartus says grudgingly, holding up the file.

Morno acknowledges the praise only slightly.

Across the great gaping mouth of the earth Tartus rides the freight elevator into the scaffolding which mirrors his own. The elevator rattles and bangs its way into the steel girders which recede within the mountain towards the giant radiation seal door. Bobcats with forklift attachments move around up here in what they call "the rafters" shuffling everything from man-high boxes of paper to extra carbide drill bits from one location to another. Tartus steps out of the way of one as it backs up and turns around.

His side of the rafters is nearly free of this kind of detritus of digging, partly because they never worried about filling out forms in triplicate back home, and the ethos has carried over, partly because the other side has made more direct progress into a deeper part of the mine. He reflects that Morno seems to love making people fill out forms. Still his system over on this side works: while items like paper and files have stayed near the offices, carbide drill bits, tungsten alloy shovels and picks and other Bobcat attachments have followed behind the digging, if well tagged to prevent losses. The losses are not from his people.

He works his way through this maze of rearranging another rearrangement, trying to keep down the feeling that he is someone's underling and should behave accordingly. He is Morno's boss here in the mine, though Morno runs this side, and Tom is his boss; things were always easier back home. Power structures were looser with people respecting elders and kings because it was the right thing to do, not because of forms and money. He didn't have to worry about giving direct orders, or issuing many proclamations. Everyone already knew. Here, people wait to be told, and life is so spread out, no one can keep everything they need to know in their heads.

Tartus grimaces as he arrives at Tom's office door decorated with children's drawings, strange figurines on his desk and shelves among the technical manuals and industrial catalogs. The figurines have giant eyes, pot bellies and purple hair standing on end. Tartus wonders if it's some sort of religious symbol. He has never had the courage to ask.

"Hey, Tartus," Tom says from his desk where he's typing.

"Tom." Tartus sits down glowering.

"Your crew is still missing in action," Tom doesn't look up from his typing.

"On behalf of them I must apologize," Tartus says, if somewhat perfunctorily. "I don't know what the authorities think we have done."

Tom stops. "Well... I think they're just being extra careful." He scratches a day's growth of beard, pitiful by diggers' standards. Tartus pushes down on the feeling of superiority he feels that the man cannot grow a proper beard. "We didn't worry much about putting you all on the project. We do check credit scores to look for responsibility, but honestly there are so many poor people out this way from LV that we weren't surprised to find half of everyone doesn't have any credit. Who needs a credit card when they don't have money? Most people get that these days, what with the card companies being what they are now. Plus, Nevada is about the only state left with any form of usury laws still on the books that haven't been totally defanged... the loan sharking from the old days of the casinos. Back when there was mafia still in town. Sorry, my wife went to grad school during the housing boom and got squeezed pretty good trying to get through. If it wasn't for some family money we would have gone under. Anyway, I understand."

Tartus tries to decipher this. "Thanks, Tom."

"Just have your people back at work ASAP. OK? The Feds will do their thing and be gone before you know it. We've been working with you guys for ages. We know you."

Tartus nods to Tom, and gets up.

"Tartus?" Tartus turns.

"We do know you, right? There's not anything you want to tell me?" The figurines look down from the bookshelves, up from the desk. A picture of Tom's daughter arranged amongst them.

"No. You know us better than anyone in Las Vegas, Tom." Tom nods, and goes back to typing. Tartus finds his way out.

Back in his office he calls several bail bonds people. He notes the Open 24 Hours in the phone book ads. He had wondered, being back on swing shift.

"I'm looking for a group rate." He keeps looking out through the glass to the office next door where Tihan should be.

A laugh. "There isn't really such a thing as a group rate." "They're being charged as a group."

"An angry mob?"

"Something like that."

"Sorry. We can't help."

Tom in his denim and blue short-sleeved collared twills across the chasm moving purposefully.

"What if I give you all of their names, can you get back to me with a bulk quote?"

"We don't bargain, Mr...?" Tartus hangs up and tries someone else.

An hour later he has a satisfactory answer. The sounds of the mine different today with so few workers.

Morno in the doorway.

"Yes?" Tartus asks formally.

"I..." Morno starts, makes a clan gesture Tartus has trouble deciphering, it could mean 'down with it' or something rude like 'fart on our relationship in this small enclosed space'. He looks at the doorframe of the glass door, the glass walls of the office and the bent blinds hanging haphazardly – nothing quite true in this prefab space built high on the cavern wall. The rafters. "I'm going to meet with Norton."

Tartus takes a moment trying to figure out what Morno, prickly and difficult, is trying to say.

"You should come with me."

They ride the tram down and out to the parking lot, and get in the LRII. Strange to have Morno here after days without any comrades. They drive back into Las Vegas in the rose sunrise.

27.

Fenur walking across the floor of the lobby. The interior a ghostly mix of electric shadows, the lofted ceiling reflecting otherworldly colors. Down at his level the ancient looking, sand colored interior buildings of the hotel, kept under glass. The pyramid a dark hum of activity after hours, a low rumble permeating down to its foundations. It makes him feel at home. Lasers shoot through the upper air and the tone of the lighting changes as the hotel exhales, its day over.

Vilhan on him before he grasps what is happening. Grabbing him from behind he pushes Fenur into one of the service alleys of the hotel. As an employee of a local hotel Vilhan seems to find this service hatch by reflex. They stand in front of one of the card keyed doors out of the way of staff and locals. Fenur recovering from the initial panic of what was once a familiar experience that often ended in a beating. His first experience of the other houses. "You will listen to me," Vilhan states, using his most lordly voice. Fenur finds himself rebelling looking for an exit to the local world before he has even registered the words.

"Or what? You will spit on me again?" Fenur offers in return.

Vilhan biting back something. "You and Tartus are correct - you owe us nothing. This is our concern: that you will leave without us." Vilhan checks around him to make sure no one is watching or listening. Another custom Fenur finds familiar.

"The underpeople would never do that. If you understood anything o them, you could see that in them."

Vilhan seems taken slightly off guard by this. Thinking, he says,"Perhaps." Thinking, he finally asks,"Have you considered... staying?" Vilhan says it in a way Fenur finds hard to read.

He tries to slow the moment down in his head. Vilhan strange, finding him here, starting without preamble.

A worker emerges from the keyed door, sees Fenur, one of their longtime residents, and says,"Sir," by way of greeting, nodding to him, moves out into the darkening lobby. This breaking into Fenur's thoughts. Initially when he arrived, he would not have understood the local social order, might have even considered asking this lowly employee for help in extricating himself from this situation with Vilhan.

After a moment, Fenur responds,"I have." He watches the lobby for moment. "I have considered staying."

"Norvil said you might have a vial of oil."

"Norvil apparently was wrong about many things. Or he would still be here."

"DO YOU-" Vilhan stops himself. "His body has gone missing. Obviously it tries to find the nearest, weakest spot between this world and home. It will try to find a way through. Do you have the oil? Can you get more? Are the underpeople making it again?"

"No." He adds,"I don't think they have the facilities."

"The pain the houses experience from being conscious, can be nothing compared to what Norvil feels - unable to reach his stasis point in the continuum in the south at the well of forgetting. But we could stay indefinitely, if-" Vilhan breaks off. "We could live forever.

"Leanor holds on to the hope we may still be able to return. If Norvil must suffer on this side so we may live, so be it. She is still an innocent. A girl. She was full of nonsense when I met her - I thought you would entertain her. That I could govern as Norton wanted. And you did entertain her. But she has not found the things most of us do as we find our way through the lifestream – it has made her irrational as a leader. If she had not been intent on governing herself... She sent you for Norton's pendant, thinking we could maintain control of his body with it. But Norvil in pain, I fear, is more than she could bear."

"That she holds hope is not something that would put her out of my favor," says Fenur, surprised that he is defending her. A sense of optimism, a lack of moral equivalency, as reason for Leanor's lunacy had not occurred to Fenur. The weight of all that has happened, and their inability to return, to eventually find rest in the long wandering of the houses – Fenur comprehending the terrible burden of it. Somewhere inside, his actions at the pass take on a slightly different meaning for him. "And I was not able to obtain the pendant."

After a moment of thinking on this, Vilhan says,"She is not the queen she should have been."

Fenur does not state what he considers obvious concerning his thoughts for Vilhan's ability to govern. At this he turns to thoughts of Norton, who he had held in slightly higher regard. Did Vilhan just implicate him in trying to undermine his daughter even as the war was starting? It had not occurred to him that perhaps he had been used as a way of blunting Leanor's grip on her throne. His estimation of Norton goes down. "She is who she is - I venture she has done far more and better than any of ...us... would have fared." He expects a retort for his efforts at including his people in this statement; a reminder of

Vilhan's station, a reminder of Fenur's past, some small... the diggers call it 'a shovel ringing off stone' - a petty reminder. Tartus' people are not without their own poetry... He's tired, having these disassociated thoughts.

Vilhan stares at the ceiling of the hotel lobby, thinking.

"Can you ask them if they can make more of the oil? What they would need?" asks Vilhan.

An affirmative gesture from Fenur. "I can."

"You are unsure."

"The oil was overseen by the mages. All of the mages studied different concepts, and had different talents. Some even know of the two points in our continuum – how we emerge from the north, and are lost in the south. They know some even of why. Yet they missed many things the locals take for granted in their technologies. Whether the remaining one knows how..."

Vilhan grimaces at this. Fenur again lowers his estimation of Vilhan. Why had it not occurred to him in all this time that Vilhan was not incisive in the way of his queen? Did Leanor find Fenur cannier? Is that what her jibes are? A kind of testing of someone else's insightfulness? After a moment's thought he asks,"Are you aging as well?"

Vilhan goes slightly stiffer, but says only,"You do have a vial." It is not a question.

To change the subject Fenur says,"I will ask Tihan - she is closest with the remaining mage. Perhaps it can be accomplished."

"We must regroup - my outburst before... was unacceptable. Norton entreated me to apologize. I apologize Fenur. We may be here forever. And we may lose ourselves in this place if we cannot find what we need here." Vilhan goes on, unable to stop himself,"But if we find what we require to live, we could also rule."

"There is no more oil," Fenur says flatly.

"You are out?" whatever little subterfuge Vilhan had in this inauthentic apology is exposed by the greed and envy in his voice.

"I had very little when we arrived. It is gone now."

"You used it to make money here." Vilhan states. Also not a question.

"Yes." Fenur feeling no shame.

"What if they need it to make more?" asks Vilhan, near panic.

"That can't be - how would the underpeople have made it for us originally?"

Vilhan seems to accept this, not having thought of it. "Yes. You... you are right. We have need of you Fenur. We all reconcile to the difficulties here in our own way. I am sorry."

Fenur makes a gesture of accepting this. Vilhan leaves him standing in the service hall without a formal goodbye. Fenur watches him wandering away, finally begins to move after him. Fenur moves to a second level of the hotel's interior, watching Vilhan make his way outside, where he sees Konor waiting for Vilhan in an older green sports car at the pick up and dropoff point. The two exchange some sort of information, and drive away.

Fenur feels something strange. Something ominous and twisting.

Fear for Leanor, and sick glee for himself.

28.

Single beam overhead LED lights illuminate the way through the snaking corridor abutting the main dig. The tunnel big enough for flatbed trucks, military vehicles. Paved unlike so much of the burial site. The passage opens up to a large room full of stacked cores of depleted uranium. Overhead, a spaceframe reinforces the ceiling. The cool temperature underground, creating condensation on the concrete underfoot, nearly slippery.

Tarnus checks logs, counts, spot checking through the cavernous room that numbers and dates on tags reconcile with logs and cores. The forms come from a place called Washington, as do the few military personnel.

After he is satisfied he continues on, deeper into this partitioned off section of the mine.

Another portal across the cavern.

Tarnus in the access tunnel headed downwards, stubby legs stumbling over the metal gratings of individual stairs. Below him an electric cog rail runs, parallel to the stairway; a loading and offloading area here at the top for the cores made below. Automatic carts clack along the railway towards the bottom. Lead plated walls line the tunnel. The LEDs flash directionally, delineating the course of cog rail travel as well as travel along the walkway. At the bottom of this tunnel a hatch below the walkway - an airlock system for the cog rail to contain a radiation leak from the lab below. The walkway attaching to an anteroom that runs over the tracks and airlock. The cog rail running directly into the area where the depleted uranium and fuel are separated from each other.

Tarnus at the lock door of the anteroom to the lab. He fishes for keys, unlocks and enters the small antechamber and is met by someone associated with the locals' military - there aren't very many of them - well-trained and essentially useless here. The diggers recognize all of them, even out of uniform. There might be twenty of them if he counts all the shifts and perimeter watch posts.

"Scheduled visit from the dig," Tarnus says to the officer.

The army officer says nothing, proffering papers. Tarnus takes the papers and begins his circuit through the separation facility. A small lab, created almost entirely of thick lead, with stainless steel reinforcing beams webbing around and through the structure. Deeper behind the protective walls somewhere, the diastolic sounds of an earthcrusher pulverizing a lode of uranium, while under it, the syncopated sound of compactification taking place. Pummeled and run through an ultrafine grating, the urnanium is forced down to widths smaller than the hairs on Tarnus' head. The uranium becoming an ultrafine dust, kept confined by the apparatus, is siphoned to separators, and sorted by a process called cryogenic distillation.

Tall tubes allow the different types of uranium, isotopes the locals call them, to settle in liquid nitrogen. The frozen isotopes weighing slightly different amounts. Frozen close to absolute zero, they float to a particular level in the liquid nitrogen tubes. The tubes rising like silos through the lab on the opposite side of this antechamber's window. The different atomic weights of the element and the offal then siphoned off, the temperature allowed to rise, the liquid nitrogen evaporating and leaving the purified forms. The dust without ever leaving the system, is then run to a compactor and formed into the long cylinders he checked above.

The depleted uranium used mainly for armament, he gathers from the television. (The locals here never talk about what they are doing). The other isotope formed into rods for energy which are shipped out, and across these foreign lands.

On one side of this guarded vestibule, supported by the stainless steel spaceframe, an armored window set into the leaded walls. Through the distorted glass rises the tall cryogenic tubes in another cavernous chamber. A fine mist of condensation from the tall tubes, cascading down below the gantry floor of the room. The mist falling from the tall cryotubes in waves past the monitors stationed along the gantries. Falling down to the cement flooring where the connective veins of wires and cabling, the injector tubes and plumbing, bring the frozen uranium dust through the system to the cryogenic tubes.

Tarnus only thinks about it in terms of production and maintenance.

Two or three people moving along the gantries, monitoring the process. Another airlock hatch to one side of the armored window, behind the military officer at his desk. A person behind the glass, the chamber behind dropping away below down flights of metal stairs, gangways following the cryo-distillation tubes back. The LED lights keep the chamber in sharp relief behind the armored leaded glass window. Tarnus theorizing the LEDs are used in place of plasma because of the dangerous microscopic dust particles.

He presses an intercom below the viewing window. The person on the other side jumps, then waves, and presses the intercom. "Yes?"

"Hey, Nod, I need a verbal positive from you on the system."

"We're functioning well."

"Thank you. See you next week."

"Have a good day, Tar." Tarnus marks the sheet and returns it to the military guard.

Takes his own copy and starts back towards his office.

29.

Mr. Tartus Mountain?" a prim looking weedy girl, with giant hair and too much make-up asks Tartus.

"Yes?" he says looking up.

"Right this way." She holds a little pass-through gate open from the outer waiting room. When she turns he notices a tattoo across the small of her back – a gateway with some species of local bird. It installs in him a sense of foreboding. The gate leads into a series of messy desks and pin-up boards featuring pictures of scary locals and police print-outs. A marker board and an overhead projector. Files upon files on desks and tired old screensavers on dated computers. The outer office held gun magazines or publications about how to hunt and fish, a few car magazines with blurbs screaming: MOST POWER FROM YOUR V8! and LIGHT RIMS!

Tartus realizes how similar to the locals on the pinup boards he and his kind look. And then that he had been reading the magazines.

The interior on the other side of the pass-through smells of burnt coffee still dripping in the back near an open door to a bathroom, stained carpet rubbed to gaping sores in some places, walls with scuff marks and ancient florescent lighting. The mine is cleaner.

A sinking feeling in Tartus.

"I'm Skip. You called about your friends? They were arrested in some sort of brawl?" asks a man in a strange haircut. It's short in the front, but hangs down nearly to his shoulders in fluffy curls in the back.

"Yes, our trailers were raided; it was some sort of mistake."

The man nods understandingly. "Some of them are being held on a few other violations we all thought had been resolved." Tartus shrugs, a theatrical gesture he has to think about, as though this answers the question.

"Yes..." the man called Skip examines a file. "Well, I called down to the city jail and asked about the address you gave, and they faxed over a list of thirty-seven names and you're right; most of these are minor - and they could use the space at the jail. But I'm worried about the amount of outlay you're facing personally to get your friends out on bond."

"I see," Tartus interjects.

"Parking tickets, driving without insurance, three assault charges in look like bar fights, at least those are slightly older..." Probably Morno or his people. They have been slowest to adjust.

"Really?" Tartus says, surprised at the timeline.

Skip looks up. "Yep. A few months old at least. Forever in outstanding warrant terms."

"Oh." Tartus recalculates how long the meshing of lifestreams has been going on. How long they have left before they truly forget.

"Are you sure you want the grand total?" Skip asks him.

Tartus nods so he doesn't seem strange.

"Forty-three-thousand nine-hundred and sixty-two." Skip looks at Tartus waiting for the fall out.

Tartus reaches into his battered trenchcoat, fishing around.

"Will you accept this as collateral?" he pulls out a piece of gold as big as his fist and puts it on Skip's desk.

The bailbondsman dumbfounded. "Is this real?"

30.

At a lodge for travelers he finds Tarnus is a pair of boxer shorts holding a weak ale, the TV blaring.

Tarnus scratches his hairy chest and leans in the doorway. Tartus leans against the railing of the motel's second floor walkway, extended over parking spaces below. The railing hot on his back.

"They don't want us, but today the mine was nearly silent. What would they do without us?"

Tarnus says nothing, seems to be half-listening to the TV.

"I need you to return with me." Tarnus frowns. "And if I don't?" is all he says.

"We really are fading."

He makes an affirmative gesture but says nothing, taking a drink of the weak ale.

"When you and Tihan were arrested for the thing at Love Jonze... after that, we've been showing up to them. Staying on their records. In their minds." "We take their money. We work their jobs. We have to eat. Eventually we become one with them. Sound familiar?" Tarnus swigging from the ale goes back inside, leaving the door open. Inside the bed is unmade, Tarnus watching pro wrestling on cable.

Tartus grabs a warm ale off a chipped dresser and sits on a chair next to the bed watching along with Tarnus. "We make our worlds in our own image."

They watch the strange men on television hitting each other while a crowd cheers. "I wonder if it's real..." ponders Tartus.

"Of course it is," replies Tarnus.

## 31.

"You like it?" asks Vertosi.

Fenur looks over the SZ. The windshield glass is perfect, the brightwork unmarred, the plastic side windows have no scuffs or aged yellow brittleness. A five-point harness and two tone cloth interior. Blue Jaeger gauges, jarring and incorrect, are set in the dash.

Vertosi continues walking around the SZ, admiring his find. "I think the guy had a wrecked 2600 somewhere he was working on - I wonder if all he could save was those gauges. Anyway, they're worth a lot - real you know? Not rebuilt or anything. That blue was one of those things they did for their Mille Miglia work. You like Mille Miglia? They said you could read them better at night and over a long period of time in the car."

"Thank you, Mr. Vertosi," Fenur says, trying to find some memory of what the Mille Miglia is, where it is.

"Well, I remembered you saying you liked the old fascistas but you couldn't find one of their cars. Sometimes there's one of the fancy ones on the market, sometimes not. One of the local classic car dealers, he's into us, and we forgave him on something. It's your payment. All you got to do is go by and sign the papers."

Fenur expresses what he hopes is taken as gratitude, something he has trouble conveying to the locals at the best of times. Even when he means it, like now. "Thank you again. I mean it."

"I know, kid. Look, I can see it's hard for you to say thank you. Nobody ever gave me nothing either. Sometimes, no one wants to give you stuff - hey, Fenur, you listening to me?" asks Vertosi abruptly.

Fenur aware it's the first time the old man has used his full name. "I'm listening, Mr. Vertosi."

"Everything go ok?" Vertosi asks carefully.

"It went ok," Fenur asserts.

Vertosi nods, seeing that Fenur is being honest, and gets what isn't said. After this, Vertosi continues,"Sometimes, nobody wants to give you nothing." And he looks Fenur in the eyes,"You take it. 'Cause that's what you got to do, you wanna live in this world." The old man appears suddenly hard and though still small, tough. "Sometimes it's the only way. And don't ever say you're sorry for doing what had to be done. You know?"

Fenur says,"I know."

"Make sure of it." Vertosi claps him on the back. Fenur takes it as a good sign.

"Thank you again."

"No problem kid. You need anything from now on, you know where to come. I'll vouch for you myself." Vertosi gives him a last slap on the upper arm with his small tanned hand. The hand remarkably hard.

The Finn who has been waiting near the porch of the house out of the sun, walks over helping Vertosi back inside.

After the Finn has seen the old man in, he returns to Fenur at the curb. "I'll return the eye-talian for you. Take the SZ out for a spin. After you sign the papers, come back and you offer to give him a ride in it. And change the dash. Probably half the money in this car is in the gauges, if you see what I'm getting at."

"I understand." Fenur makes a mental note.

"I know you're thinking we stiffed you, it can't be more than seventy five grand all told, but it's hard goods. It's a gift. No tax problems, no nothing. Plus there's something for you in the trunk. From Sato's people. Don't try and register it. It's an heirloom of one of their emperors and will come up on one of those art police watch lists. Ok?"

Fenur tries to absorb this. "I think I understand."

"You better, man, it would be hard to explain. I don't even want to know what you want it for." The Finn laughs at his own joke. "No, you don't," Fenur says solemnly.

The Finn looks him over. "Fee, pick up Sato and take him to the airport. That's the last part of this. If anybody bothers you about it just say he was a guy from a card game - he did well, he tipped you well, you're just seeing him off. Just another Japanese business guy who wanted to see Vegas."

"I got it." Fee opens the door to the SZ; the door is lighter than the V6's. The key fits snugly into the dash, a crisp clicking. The engine comes to life in a higher, nearly whiny voice. Fenur smiles up at the Finn. "Say thanks to him again for me."

"I will," replies the Finn, and closes the car's door for him.


32.


Tihan awake from a dream about the steam tubes deep beneath the mountains. Geothermal taps and underground rivers harnessed by the underpeople. She has the sound of them in her bones. The pressure of the steam vibrating the rock in harmonies somewhere below hearing, then pushing up into the audible as her location in the mines would change, the curls of steamtubing heating and powering the mines, the many bends tuning the sounds from within the pipes. Warmth and locomotion. Another sound mixing with those of the dig, always the dig.

"What were you thinking about?" asks Hano, preparing a more sophisticated tool.

"The steam in the mines," she says pouring another cup of coffee from a carafe of the burnt liquid. "How old is this coffee?"

Hano looks up. Shrugs and goes back to work.

Tihan looks at the brew, sniffs, drinks it anyway.

"Have to stay warm somehow!" says Hano joking about the hot work of carrying temperature regulation and light to the rest of the underground cities. "The garbage men, the torchmen and those that deal with the shit: those are the people with real power. No one wants to climb down into a sewer to fix their toilet, or to categorize their refuse. But someone has to. I always liked the 'toss it in the earth's blood' solution." For the phrase he reverts to their own language.

"They call it lava here." "Do they? Why?" scoffs Hano.

"Something scientific."

"Oh, of course. Science." Hano looks at her playfully, back on the subject of the locals and their beliefs.

"They are fools – they have traveled further than us, to other worlds, and then don't believe they have done it. They make this filth they need to cover in the earth – then Tartus fights their fight for them, trying to protect them from themselves. They build this -rubbish- it accumulates around them everywhere and they ignore it. Science is for the wise, I would tell them." Tihan says to his look.

"Why we should stick to 'magic'! ...Perhaps. More knowledge, less wisdom. Look at the way they use oil - we refined it and sold it to the houses. Ridiculous to power a world with it. Ugh."

"They say the material they bring to the mine is even worse..." She takes another sip, Hano not responding immediately. "I am sorry for what happened to your wife," Tihan offers into the pause as Hano considers the direction the conversation has led. "The oil reminded me."

Hano makes a motion of assent. "I should not be so opposed to the process of making the oil. But, she... it reminds me. She would have approved of their concept – the leftovers that Tartus deals with out there – it did not occur to her."

For a moment Hano looks small, old, and broken. Then he seems to come to life again, continuing on with the same conversation,"But we used root spirits for lubrication of the machines, rubber from plants for insulations. They have improved upon it."

"I'm not arguing."

"You are." Hano stops. "I still don't understand what happened at the well of ice, though I have heard the chronicle recounted many times. The – lava – explosion. And what was buried there making its way out after being frozen for so long. Norton, Konor and Morno were lucky to survive. If you can call it luck. How could we have no record of the accumulation? The locals have no explanation either – they have no corollary."

"No... But the accumulation wouldn't seem scientific to them. Although look at their world – the way the buildings have all started to look alike. The peoples' dress. Their thoughts from the... the... computers."

"It accumulates into one thing. One way. Dangerous."

"The scientists here call it 'monoculture.'"

Hano rummages through old electrical equipment. "A system seems like an answer. A placement of things seems like a – what? What was it called?" He asks, blanking on the locals' word for a moment. "A system is not a science. A zoo! That's what they call it! Although their science is a system. Categorizing... As though that makes life simpler. Perhaps they are wrong to think that it works always."

"Still, they go faster, their ability to communicate over distance is superior-"

Hano talking off-handley as a solder heats up. "And they can't hear the stars for all the noise they have generated doing it."

"And we barely grasp what they mean by this communication. Can you picture a New York or Venice?"

"I've seen it downtown."

"The real ones." "Who cares? They rebuilt them here. They're probably the same.

That's the point, isn't it?"

"What if it's not?" she asks.

"That doesn't make any sense! Who would build a thing like another thing that was meant to be different! That's lunacy!" Hano finishes soldering a rack o tube sockets, capacitors and resistors into a rusty steel box he had found lying in a dank end of the shop. "These are octals, these are inverters, these are inputs. He points at double rows of where the tubes fit into the chassis, marking of each in turn. "Find the tubes I need in that drawer over there, and measure them to make sure they are vacuum sealed still and will draw current readily Then find two more sets and pack them so they are neatly accessible. My rough measurements- tell me the place where we opened –the weakness between- i moving. We will go to the dig. And this time I will bring a metering device fo the electricity."

"One of us needs to call Tartus to get you a security clearance card for th mine." Tihan adds.

"Do that too. I have books to check. I will show you when I have reached conclusion."

33.

The sound of jetwash, a feeling more than something audible, pushes down at Fenur as he walks back across the parking lot of the airport. After he had deposited the Japanese katana at the hotel, he had picked up Sato, driven him here, and left him at the entry gate.

Sato on the curb. A bow with no words, a faint half-smile perhaps.

Fenur wasn't sure.

Fenur thinking about the sword, returning to his suite, when a hand grabs him from behind, rumpling the expensive material of his suit, wadding it under hand and shoving him into the door of the SZ. A blur as Fenur tries to get a look at who is behind him - an airport security car, two other cars, large and non-decript. He has forgotten the oil for several days; he had nearly become one of these local people. Walking and thinking of something else. And he completely missed these ...men... pulling up behind him. Official looking people stepping onto pavement, surrounding him.

"That was funny," says the man, forcing Fenur's head down against the roof of the car. "We got your friend inside. A badge flops open next to where his head is being pressed. "You see that?" The man takes a handful of Fenur's hair forcing him to look at the badge, "You know what that says?"

"FBI?" asks Fenur. He sees the man's name: Scasey. Again.

"That's right." Scasey cuffs Fenur, head still on the SZ.

He saw this man emerge from Leanor's office before his first visit with her in so long. When the dark mead was left for him at his hotel suite. "I see why Leanor wanted a restraining order," Fenur says blandly.

"That's right." Scasey cuffs Fenur, and turns him around. "You know what that badge means? It means I can do anything I want to you. You're scum, and everyone knows it. If you disappear off this spot and you are never seen again, no one is going to care." Scasey whips Fenur around.

Fenur sensing the heat of the car roof, an actual realization that it's uncomfortable, radiating up into his skull, his tolerance for temperature at its limit.

"How much do you think it was worth?" Scasey asks.

Fenur says nothing, sensing what is coming. Pushed back against the car, he is off balance, something the houses used to use when they wanted one of their trophies to feel powerless.

Scasey barely controlling himself. "My wife won't even go back to the house!" He stops for a moment, then shouts:"She's taken my boys!"

Fenur a mask.

"We know all about the money laundering through the exotic car shop," Scasey continues. He opens the door of the SZ and looks inside theatrically, as though he already knows what he will find. "Jaeger gauges, wow; those must be worth a fortune." He pronounces it differently from Vertosi; saying it Yayger. He takes a foot and kicks the dash shattering one of the blue gauges. "Not really correct for the car though – were you going to sell them, and replace them?"

Fenur remains impassive, stoic as a slave.

"I know it was you. I know that Japanese goon and you were at my house." Scasey kicks out the other gauge. "I have the security footage from the mall. We've been following Sato and the Yakuza for years. How stupid are you?" He grabs Fenur's head again and slams him backwards into the SZ leaving a dent in the side of the coupe. The man shorter than Fenur; he has to reach up for the handful of hair. The whole thing ridiculous and awkward. "There's your payment. Tell the old bastard what it's worth now when you see him."

Fenur stares into Scasey's eyes. He sees his past reflected in this strange foreign man.

"Nothing to say?" Scasey slams Fenur's head against the roof of the car again.

"Jack, that's enough," says one of the other men standing a little further back.

Reeling, Fenur is pushed forward at the other men by Scasey. "Fine - you take him." Scasey storms away. Fenur stumbles, the others steadying him, putting him in the back of one of the official looking cars, pushing him down and inside the doorsill.

34.

He's awake again, sitting in a cell in something on the ride over they referred to as the federal building, waiting. No sign of Sato – he must have made his plane. Scasey lying or officials on the other end of the flight dealing with the yakuza.

The smell of the underpeople strange but not as strange as here; he especially notices the way the locals smell in confined spaces. Their lives moaning through the concrete and steel. He was dreaming of... ...he was dreaming of the invasion. That's what it was. Again. Always somewhere back in his dreams the moment of the beginning. The explosion at the well of ice and the plague, Norton, Konor and Morno driven before it.

One of the uniformed men approaches his cell.

Standing at a phone in the holding area. Mostly being left alone by the other detainees. He dials a number for the Finn's emergency throw-away.

Fenur says,"It's me." "Who is that?" asks the Finn.

"Something has happened." Fenur lets the warning hang.

"I'm sorry, pal. You've got the wrong number." The phone goes dead. Fenur wonders if he heard a note of fear in the Finn's voice.

He arrives at the other side of the bulletproof glass. Despite the rough treatment he looks the same; immaculate in torn clothes. A blue uniformed man hands Fenur a manila envelope and a pair of black shoelaces. He doesn't make eye contact with her as he waits, signs a piece of paper on a clipboard, even as the door buzzes him out of a holding area. He waits while she hands over papers, signing documents, pressing a black credit card to the papers while she reads. The police say nothing during the process.

"Never seen a card like this before," says the policeman who processes him out. Leanor says nothing, taking back the card, paying the bond in silence.

Fenur can think of nothing to say all the way across to a parking lot. The air heavy with the thick taste of a storm.

"I'm sorry, I didn't..." Fenur stops. Rain beats on the roof made of British aluminum. The defogger set on high, Leanor staring out the windshield. "I tried Tartus first."

Leanor twisting into something wry and sad. "Of course you did." She keeps staring forward, far away. "I hate the desert," she says, nearly to herself. "It never rains here, and then when it does it's torrential."

"The underpeople are under suspicion as well," Fenur tries to explain, ignoring her.

Continuing, she asks him,"Remember the rain in the forests? Remember how gentle it was? Nearly mist. If it hadn't been for the underpeople our armors would have rusted away. We traded with them, and though we did not like them, we respected them as near equals." Fenur suddenly more formal in the passenger seat. She frowns at the unintended consequence of what she has said. She continues, trying to explain it away,"That night when we arrived back in the forests... After Vilhan gave you to me... When you first removed my armor... ...and showed me the custom of the people of the Far Sea... I should not have ...punished you afterwards. After want..." She adjusts the fan on the car, trying to find the resolve to continue. "I didn't understand what was happening between us. Or what it was – Vilhan gave you to me as a kind of pet, and I didn't grasp what it was – the things you were doing. I didn't know... we have trusted the emergence from the north... And you were so different. There were expectations of me then."

"No driver?" he asks, trying to hurt her. To interrupt her reverie.

"I didn't think they needed to know every aspect of my personal life."

"Still the queen," Fenur mumbles. "As though there are no expectations of you now." She has no response. When she does not rise to this he lets a moment pass and finally says,"I didn't want to call you. Tartus..." He steels himself,"Thank you for bailing me out."

Leanor inscrutable. She asks,"When you saw him leaving my office, had you encountered him already?"

Fenur makes an affirmative gesture. "Scasey?"

"Yes. After the dark mead was sent to you."

"No. Our conversation then... It took some time for me to discover its loft within my thoughts," Fenur says.

She smiles. "You translate the sayings of the Far Sea people into English? They sound so quaint."

"It reminds me," he explains, reticent to give her this, to let go of it.

"Do you miss the balloon ships and the ice of the Far Sea? We speak in English as a matter of habit." And then she continues by saying what both of them are thinking:"And because you hate to listen to the other houses in their dialect. I think you grew to prefer the sound of the underpeoples' tongue."

"Perhaps," he replies. A sullenness that's barely hidden.

She seems slightly diffident, or as though she is waiting, trying to decide on something. "In some ways you and they are probably closer to the origins than the ...other... houses." She corrects herself almost imperceptibly, so as to include the people of the Far Sea.

"You said we sounded like animals. Worse than the claypeople, you said."

Again the sad smile. After a time she reaches over pushing herself against him, soft and slightly damp, raising the memories of home.

"Closer to the origins like the accumulation."

She stops him, kisses his neck, pushing against him. "Please forgive me," she whispers. He tries to pull away, tensing. "I didn't... I should have had you as my king after Vilhan's betrayals of our kinds. It is not fair that he survived while the Far Sea people did not. You did what I could not. I never... I regret that I could not. You cannot know the difficulty of living with my inaction. I should have been able to say it." She pushes a hand under his torn shirt. "To order it ...and Vilhan. Fenur forgive me, I still love you."

He sits, tense against her, sad and waiting. "I don't know, Lea." But he reaches up, cups her cheek and presses her to him. "If you had ordered it... I would have had to refuse."

"Perhaps then we would have died as befitted us." Time passes while they remember each other, and while the idiosyncrasies of what they are play out against each other as physical space. Eventually she says, "The underpeople still believe the oil has no effect on us," she says continuing her reminiscence of the time before. "They will be proven wrong in time, yet we cannot cross back."

He quietly assents, but then hearing something in her voice: "Risking your temper, I ask: We cannot, or we should not, cross back?"

Slowly she begins, "I do not believe we should return. To do so would mean certain death, but if we survived, the struggle between the houses and clans would begin again. Perhaps more intensely." She whispers, "We cannot leave them here in their current state after all they have done for us, when they had little reason. We must band together now. Scasey has been pressuring me for some time, and has designs on the underpeople and their dig as you say you suspected. It seems he is only a soldier in a wider war. But I do not believe he will stop until he is satisfied."

Fenur smells her damp hair, and she listens to the sounds from his chest. Leanor confides her secret to him, "And I have trouble within the houses. I was angry with you for accusing me of sending you the dark mead. Of shouting at me in front of others - the king of the underpeople no less. I don't know what would have happened if I had not thrown you from the gathering." She laughs quietly against him. "I believe I know where it originated. I will do my duty as queen to insure our survival. But, Fenur, lovely Fenur who I have hurt so with my ignorance. With my arrogance. I must ask you for your help: you must find an arrangement that prevents Scasey from engaging us, if he won't forget us as these local people have until now. For all our sakes. Or, if it is too dangerous, prevail upon the underpeople to do so." She stops, gauging, then adds,"Or your other contacts. It is the only way we will survive."

Fenur thinks on this. "I will try, Leanor."


35.


"Hey, Fee, the important thing: Sato got on the plane, and the yaks are happy, the Finn at the pay phone of the diner he frequents.

Fenur can hear dishes, orders being taken, conversations in the background

"Scasey-" The Finn cuts him off:"First, not on the phone, right? Second Don't worry about it. Any more trouble and it's taken care of. Unless something happens sooner. You played it exactly right. If it comes to it, that's what the other kind of throw-aways are for, ok?"

"I got it." Fenur rests his forehead on the window of the suite, looking out at the airport. Planes taxiing. Blinking blue lights. The constant dance of travel "He has family. You're the one telling me family is the most important thing."

"It is. A lot of guys do. Have family. They have to provide for those families And they aren't hurting anybody. Unlike a guy who bounces your head off the hood of a car. We run a clean business. The yaks have a problem, we help them out – but we don't do that kind of thing unless we get pushed. Hard."

"Yeah..." Fenur finding it hard to argue with the logic of the man.

"Fee? It's not your problem. Understand?"

"I understand." "Are we ok on that first thing with our Yak?"

"Yes."

"It wasn't that guy – what was his name? I know you're still thinking it was us and that we made you do it. Yeah?" the Finn edging him where he doesn't want to go.

"Yeah." Fenur in a sudden burst of courage,"Yeah. I guess that is what I think."

"You sure he wasn't something to you? You say, if he was."

"No. He was nothing to me."

"We heard he got killed. But he owed us money. He was always going to owe us money, the kind of money he owed. We could have leveraged that guy he worked for, he owed us so much. Remember what LV said about the Rembrandts? He wasn't kidding around. The old man has good taste. And that's the kind of money we're talking about. We didn't want him dead – we wanted him alive. In fact, we'd like to know who made him not alive. So keep your ear to the ground – there might be something in it for you."

"Ok," Fenur using the locals terms, wondering if he knows who is responsible.

"You strike me as guy who maybe knows more than they're saying. We'll work out payment, you know?"

Fenur saying,"Maybe. Let me check on a few things."

"Get the SZ fixed and stop by and see Lou, ok?" the Finn chides him.

"I will." The Finn hangs up.

Fenur leans down placing the phone back in its cradle. He likes to carry the phone around the suite placing it at the end of its umbilical, rearrange the chair in front of the window where he can watch the planes, or in front of his music system. Circling in his tiny orbit, with constant access to the concierges of the various hotels, he has never had need of a cell phone.

Behind him the spray of water as the bath cascades out and down the tiers, recirculating. Little diamond droplets in sprays, sprays of freckles. Leanor nude, rising from the bath and padding over to him at the window. She puts her arms around him from behind leaning against him, head over his shoulder. "I see why you live here now," she says, watching the view.

"It's a big world. I wonder where they all go?" he asks vacantly, half to himself, about the planes.

She nods into his shoulder. "Your people and flight," changing the subject, and commenting on his phone call she asks,"Did you say something about Norvil?"

"No - it was just something about Stephen's card game."

Leanor presses herself against him, her tall and sharp body against the robe he wears.

"I don't want to go home, Leanor."

"I know. You are nearly the king you should have been here. If you were to forget what happened... To lose yourself in time, to not re-merge with the stream in the south... I see that for you it would be a kind of balm. To simply fade. What did your people think of the fading?"

"That it was natural."

"Natural like this – this thing you taught me. Instead of the way the houses of Nor and Vil accept the emergent ones from the north, and discern them as family. From somewhere and sometime ... before. Instead, the Far Sea people did what was natural - making new ones this way." Every bit of her, each arc and bump, pith and nub, each mottling of skin and statuesque ridge converging on his will.

"They said it was like you had given yourself to a beast. Had shamed the true houses." Fenur trying to reject her.

"They seem so trivial and petty now, don't they?" a slight laugh into his shoulder,"Your people remembered what we had forgotten. And it is so much better. I wonder-" she stops not finishing the thought, then continues in a different direction,"To fade on this side would be the same for you as on the other. As long as Vilhan lives you could not be king, perhaps not even after. It could never be there. Except among your people, who would have had you. They who are gone."

He reflects this may be the first wholly honest thing she has ever said to him. Whispering she pleads,"I know you can never love me. But have me." She unties his robe from behind and turns him, intent for him to press her naked, palms first, against the glass.

36.

"Tartus, come down here!" shouts Hano. Miners turn and look, continue along their paths into the mine.

"He won't hear you," advises Tihan.

"Call him down."

Tihan grabs her walkie—talkie. "Tartus?"

A moment then the walkie-talkie squawks back, a fizzed-out gurgle.

"It's me and... Hano."

"We have arrived!" shouts Hano pointlessly, after she has taken her finger off the talk button.

Through the walkie-talkie: "So come up."

Hano frowns at her. "He can just as well come down here." "He's afraid of the elevator," she returns into the black box.

"I am not-"

The walkie-talkie fizzes back,"I'm coming down." A few boring minutes watching the elevator ascend and descend. Hano agitated and unwilling to admit a fear of heights or the elevator.

"For someone who grew up in Wind's Breath, a fear of heights is a bit odd."

"I'm over it," Hano says defensively.

"Mmm," she rejoins unconvincingly.

Tartus picking his way through the digging machinery, aligned in rows, coded, using a complex system of access with parts seemingly dropped randomly. Each digging machine and its extras laid out according to how often it will be used.

"Welcome," Tartus greets them, stopping in front of them.

"A lot has happened since we were together last, hasn't it?"

Tihan asks Tartus. "I heard some of it as we arrived."

Tartus turns to Hano. "You wouldn't come up-" "It's not that I don't want to go up there." Hano defensive.

Tartus makes a noncommittal noise.

"It's that the contraption uses their ways." He looks sidelong at the locals who work oblivious.

"It works just as well," says Tartus tiredly.

"Can't be safe," Hano argues. "Any proper mine uses steam pneumatics."

Tartus waits.

"We need access to the dig for testing," Hano says changing the subject while not acknowledging his own idiosyncratic fears.

"Alright," Tartus scratches his beard. To Tihan he says,"Get him a pass-"

This is interrupted by another walkie-talkie blip. Tartus answers, pressing down the speak button. "Go ahead."

"We have a body down here, Tartus."

"Injured miner evac protocol," Tartus intones by wrote.

"It's not a miner. And they aren't injured." The voice has a local's accent and speech patterns - one of the foremen. "I - I don't know quite what to make of it."

"I'm coming down." Tartus turns to Hano. "Wait here." After a moment adding,"Let's not deviate. Start the injured miner protocols."

Hano more agitated. "No. I'm not waiting among these people." Tihan seeming embarrassed next to this outburst from Hano.

"Many of them are our people."

"I'm not waiting here. If you want my help, I'm coming with you."

Tartus ponders this. "Alright then."

They catch a ride on one of the mine's interior shuttles, taking the strip of black top road into the mine's interior. Giant trucks full of broken rock, shale and mud rumble past them in the opposite direction, light cutting though the grit in the air of the mine. The two story diesel engines are deafening on the dirt road next to the shuttle lane. Branches of the mine twist by as they wind deeper within.

Above them airlocks of foreign substance and steel webs. Behind these are tunnels housing the waste which is delivered nearly daily from the outside world. Giant copper tubes, porous, receding into earth, tamped in place by the underpeople and the locals' machines.

The porous copper allowing the cooling of spent fuel, absorption of radiation into the clay of the desert. Cranes float overhead on a gimble system, moving along tracks, through the main airlock, carrying sealed cargo containers from the unloading area at the mine entrance. Lights flick on and off in the dark as movement sensors pick them out, pick out the cranes moving. As airlocks open and close, waste products are deposited for the sleep of storage, the mine continuing to live and breathe and grow, worming its way deeper into the earth.

At the end of an unworked corridor they find the body suspended under bright light. Norvil's body, arc lights casting harsh shadows against the freshly cut wall, fate, or incomplete fate, in sharp relief. Tartus tries to decide as the four stare down at the unblemished body.

"I don't know if it's a crime scene or what. We don't know how he got in - nobody saw him, and here he lays." Tartus remembers the foreman's name is Bull. Tartus has never thought to ask him about this.

"The guy seems to have made his way in here past security gates, all the way down the mine and then just dropped dead, or one of the miner's killed him and somehow snuck him in here without anybody else seeing. I just don't understand it, Tartus, it's the damnedest thing

I ever did see."

Tartus looks at Norvil, leans down, and examines him, not touching. His pendant in place.

"Better not touch him, if you know what I mean," Bull says.

Tartus says,"I know, but thanks for the reminder, Bull."

Norvil's body jerks. His eyes open, and he begins to claw towards the wall. Bull, a large man, screams in a high-pitched voice and runs into the dark back towards light. They hear his shrill screams echoing back to them in the dark.

"Tihan-" says Tartus trying to suppress the jerking body.

Eyes empty.

"Grab the pendant!" growls Hano, trying to push against the torso. The body claws a finger into the freshly hewn wall. A moment of something? A smell, a feel, a type of light, something just on the edge of consciousness, of reason... The pendant snaps off in Tihan's hand.

She curses and drops it. "It was cold." The cold ground of the dig steams around the pendant.

"From whence they emerged," Hano says. He finds a piece of leather in an interior pocket, reaches out and scoops the pendant from the ground.

"But you stopped him! The way back must be right here-" she shouts.

"And so are they, I don't need the instruments from the car to tell that. And neither should you," Hano glowers. "Are you ready to merge with the accumulation?"

She looks at the wall, back at the body. "No." She sits down dejectedly staring at the claw mark on the wall. "Of course not."

Tartus pats her shoulder. "I must call Leanor." To Hano he says,"I suppose you aren't going to bother to test now."

Hano agrees.

He walks into the dark away from the arc lights. He adds,"I should also reassure our foreman Bull."


## 37.


The helicopter pad lights glower against the desert sky.

A local looks to Tartus for confirmation and Tartus affirms with a local's gesture of nodding his head.

"Sir, I have to remind you, this is a violation of about ten different kinds of laws, letting them in here like this. You could be let go; Washington won't see this as a kind of game. And none of us want to see that happen."

"Thank you for your concern," Tartus returns, watching the night sky. "I understand."

The helicopter, unseen and unheard at first, crosses into the restricted airspace of the dig. Black against a dark sky it finally takes on detail as it crosses closer and hovers above the helipad. The hotel's name written on its side: Vilhan's workplace. It deposits three tallish figures in the landing zone who are met by mine transport workers, who hurry them off the pad, out from under the whirling blades, shadows blotting out the arc lights.

"We're ready for the second one," says the local. "Are you sure about this?"

Tartus is not sure. He is also unaccustomed to having his decisions directly questioned. But the miner means well - he's asking out of concern for Tartus and concern for the mine, and Tartus sees the use in this. Everything the diggers have built is being put in jeopardy by violating the locals' rule about airspace. He says again to be clear, and to take responsibility as king,"I'm well aware of the consequences, Tim: continue."

Norton, Vilhan and Konor up a flight of steel stairs to the shipping container acting as control tower: plasma torched, windows cut into the steel a place for an air conditioning unit, wires: the giant metal box converted for use. A box for cables jut from its side, snaking down the 1500 feet or so to the bass of the mountain, where they join the main infrastructure. The mountain continues upward, compacted earth creating the landing zone, the slightly elevated makeshift control tower, close to the mouth of the dig, but not too close. A short walk down and around the curve of the mountain spine, another flight of stairs into the main complex at the mouth of the dig. From here the air traffic is directed. They hardly ever use the helipad; it's mainly for officials from far away who demanded it be built for their convenience.

"Greetings, Tartus, we are most glad to meet again and be warmly received after the rancor of our previous parley," says Konor formally on behalf of Vilhan and Norton, who hold their own counsel.

"The underpeople are glad to receive the people of the houses however we may. Our bond is a great one, and not subject to petty disagreements. Despite our past differences, we have too long now been friends," Tartus says. More personally, he asks,"Tarnus had no trouble contacting you?"

"No... We maintain a level of vigilance regarding return – we have conveyed to the locals around us the necessity of – what do they call it here? – an open door policy. Tarnus was put straight through. And I am grateful that you have communicated to us the location of the one who has been lost," says Norton, avoiding the use of Norvil's name as is their tradition when speaking of the fallen.

"I am grateful as well that we were called," adds Vilhan insincerely, but trying for ambassadorial.

Tartus tries to accept the words, knowing the desperation of the houses, and believing they desire to acquit themselves well for their people, saying,"It is good the hotels have access to helicopters."

Vilhan confirms,"Yes. Our fleet at the hotel is useful, though I have never taken advantage of it before."

"The others have been called. They are traveling by their own means. Your message was clear."

"Yes. We must speak with Hano the mage."

The air traffic controller glances up at this but is too busy conducting the landing of the second helicopter to pay attention.

Below, Leanor and Fenur disgorged onto the helipad by one of Leanor's hotel helicopters. Fenur with the katana slung over his back.

"Come; let us meet them," says Tartus and heads out and down away from the control tower, his beard jumping as his short legs catch the stairs beneath him.

Less formally, and out of earshot of the air traffic controller, he says,"The medical team on site is very sophisticated – but he appears dead. We made sure our own medics were used. There was an incident with one of our local foremen. We are not allowed to move his body."

"Does his body continue to try and break through?" asks Norton.

"We have his pendant, and our medics are watching him," trying to keep this knowledge from affronting them, Tartus continues rapidly,"An ambulance has also been called. They will not understand what has happened, but it will be yet another..." Tartus starts to say defect - the closest thing he can think of in the language, the home word meaning metallurgical defect, conscious that this would be a wrong usage, says,"...thing we must explain away. We do not have much time before they arrive. The only bit of lode struck is that they said they would not send one of these helicopters for a dead body. If your people are driving... we may need to hold the point of crossover." He stops for a moment.

Leanor and Fenur, having crossed over to the tower control box, wait at the bottom of the stairs, overhearing the last part of this. "This may be difficult," Leanor says, with a trace of her angry humor.

Fenur in Leanor's company a source of concern to Tartus.

"Greetings," Leanor adds.

"Greetings, Queen of Nor," Tartus says, hoping the phrasing communicates something to Vilhan, Norton and Konor. Tartus extends a hand of friendship, which Leanor takes.

Further away, at the main complex, Hano and Tihan over by the roadster unloading the large crate of dark mead. Next to it a measuring device jutting with tubes of Hano's own design.

Tarnus inside seeing to the operation of the mine, and to the frightened mine worker.

The eyes of the taller ones following the unloading of the crate as they make their way back down into the parking lot. Hano and Tihan find their way over through cliffs of digging machines, rock piles and snakings of lines.

"Is there oil?" asks Vilhan.

Tartus looks up at this. "No."

"Could it be made?" Vilhan continues doggedly as they approach Hano. Then by way of explanation,"This place. It feels more unstable to us."

Fenur looking to Tartus unable to communicate what has happened. Tartus remembering missed phone calls and messages that needed checking.

Hano begins without any formalities or preamble,"We may return. Perhaps the accumulation has consumed itself. Although at the site it did not feel so." Hano changes subjects without any preface or skip in rhythm. "We must find a way to open the portal in a controlled way, and push Norvil through, then try and hold it open whatever awaits us on the other side, while our kinds cross. Or we must remove him from the area as quickly as possible. We risk an opening without control the nearer he stays to the location. However, I believe his body will find its way back and try to break through again."

Fenur smiles at Hano's breach of etiquette in his way of discussing the body, it making the others of his kind so uncomfortable.

"But the portal moves," says Norton.

"Yes, and his body will try in different locales, as our worlds shift against each other. It will be more difficult for us to find each time."

A moment while they all think. "What if we destroy the body?" Leanor finally asks, sounding sick.

"Impossible," says Norton, giving her a look of revulsion. "A sort of profanity-" he cannot finish.

"No. It is a necessary question," Hano interjects. The houses look at him in horror. Leanor vindicated, though not in the eyes of her own people.

Tihan says after a moment,"It could reconstitute itself. Over time. And the problem would remain, or possibly, if we have not faded, our heirs and the houses would have the problem but understand it less."

Hano agreeing with this. "It is more dangerous to pass it forward," he says. With this he takes the pendant from his cloak. "Norvil's," Hano says, presenting it, correctly, to Leanor.

Norton starts at this, and opens his mouth to say something.

"What do you have to say, father?" asks Leanor.

Norton makes a dismissive gesture.

Leanor asks in an even sharper tone,"What would you have us do if you were king?"

Norton furious, saying nothing.

Through gritted teeth Konor says,"If he were king we would not be here now."

"And if you had let me rule in his stead-" Vilhan adds.

"No." She says, silencing debate. "We would be DEAD."

Vilhan rejoining,"You cannot know that, girl – we would not have been driven to Kragsteeth. Nor would we-"

Tartus interjects,"You were driven to Kragsteeth by the accumulation. Leanor was the one who saw through to asking for help. It is not weakness to ask for something from others when you have no other option. Whatever your own feelings about the need itself." Vilhan, Konor and Norton turn to Tartus. "She is right. This madness must stop – drop it in a bottomless hole. Be done with it."

"Stupid girl..." Vilhan says.

Leanor smacks him. "Say it again. I will have your pendant."

Fenur smiles a small smile. Tartus sees it and thinks it one of the first true smiles he has seen on the boy. Tihan with a sideways glance at Fenur. Tartus feeling sorry for her heart.

Tartus begins to attempt to smooth over Hano's roughness when he is interrupted by Tim over the walkie-talkie, from above still in the air traffic booth. "Tartus, another bird." Meaning helicopter, Tartus translates to himself. Tim adds,"FBI Agent Jack Scasey."

"Do not give them clearance to land," Tartus shouts up at Tim the controller, remembers the walkie-talkie, and repeats the command.

"They have an override they have already used. It checks out,"

Tim sounding apologetic through the static. "Sorry." "It's a federal site, Tartus..." Tihan says quietly.

The group turns and looks to the horizon watching the government helicopter come in, replacing the one from Leanor's hotel, which has lifted off.

Tartus's walkie-talkie squawks at him again, Tarnus saying over it,"Are they here?"

"Everyone has arrived. Scasey is landing also," Tartus returns into the black box.

"Scasey?"

"With a security override."

"Everyone else needs to get down here - especially Hano and

Tihan. Something's happening."

Tartus hails an electric cart. Nusmo at the wheel. "Hello, Tartus," he says, jocular in the face of the dark setting.

Leanor and Fenur hop onto the back, while Vilhan and Konor squeeze into the rear seat. Norton takes the passenger seat while Tartus drives. He looks over his shoulder at Scasey's approaching helicopter as he drives away.

"We'll follow you in," says Hano, seeing the lack of space on the cart. Hano in the roadster with Tihan. "Wait," he says getting out and opening the rear hatch of the car. "The dark mead." Tihan jumps back out and they wrestle the crate back into the rear of the car.

The cart descends into the mine on a whisper of DC power, followed by vintage Japanese bark. As soon as they are inside Hano starts with the horn, echoing off the walls of the interior cavern. The other's grit their teeth while Tartus makes an exasperated expression with his body language.

38.

Beyond the seal of the great wall, they find a few of the underpeople wrestling with the body of Norvil again. "It moves," says Tarnus. "We turn away and it moves."

"That shouldn't-" Norton starts.

Tarnus continuing,"It can't be stopped." And then to Tartus,"The humans are afraid. I can't even find one local miner remaining right now."

Norton makes a sign.

Leanor looks at the body of her brother in distress. "It feels its reunion with ime in the south," she says.

The walls of the dig chamber seem hot. Norvil's body different, look away. Back. Placement changed. Scrabbling sounds under artificial illumination. The diggers dragging the body away from its trajectory again. The taller ones looking away from what they consider taboo.

Fenur examining the body, thinking, and finally putting out a foot, and pressing down on the body's outreached hand quietly vibrating with energy, pointing at an axe mark on the wall some feet away.

Tartus pocketing two of the bottles of mead. Holding a third.

"Norvil, if you are in there, return to us." The body lies still. Unresponsive.

"Norvil, there is mead and there is oil. Arise, and be whole again, if you can," Tartus implores the apparition on the floor.

"The continuum requires him to merge," Vilhan says.

"Even oil would salve it no longer," Norton says.

"How does the oil work?" Hano asks.

The taller ones refuse to answer.

"What is in the south?" Hano asks even more archly.

Tartus pours the mead on Norvil.

"Tartus..." Fenur starts. "He was in the morgue. They pronounced him dead."

"THEY DO NOT UNDERSTAND WHAT WE ARE!" Norton roars.

"They would understand on examination," Fenur returns.

Norton in a lower voice,"It is forbidden to go there." Norton tentatively feeling the wall where the barrier is thin.

"There are no stories?" Hano incredulous, watching him.

"There are." The tone would normally cut off conversation on the subject.

Leanor offers,"It is similar to the well of ice. A kind of stasis point. Everything slows to a stop. It is painful to exist in time for us. They say as you walk, the world slows to a stop but you are unaware. It feels as though it goes on forever. We say it is the well of forgetting."

"Has anyone ever been there and returned?" Tihan asks, seeing the direction of Hano's thoughts.

"There are myths. But no, not in recorded history."

"None who's pendants rot and fall have returned?"

Leanor says nothing. Then,"It is an abomination. We do not allow it. Do you understand?"

The body continues to struggle towards the wall.

"The well of ice erupted when prodded." Hano suggests.

"THEY ARE NOT THE SAME!" Norton roars.

"A flux in time could have allowed a huge amount of energy to-" Hano begins to explain. "A kind of loop. Your exploration of the north could have caused the loop to flux. It could explain the accumulation."

"NO." Norton shouts. "IT COULD NOT."

Leanor with a positive expression. "It could."

Scasey suddenly, comically, on a whisper quiet electric cart storms into the dig chamber. Jumping from the cart he has commandeered, interrupting them, interjecting into this:"-You thought you could walk away from me and I would just wait up top?" Scasey nearly shouting at Tartus. The group stops, his abrupt entrance breaking the moment.

Tartus turns, looks down, gives the body of Norvil a moment's consideration.

The rest of the group shocked by the intrusion of the man.

Scasey says, sounding pedantic,"I'm from Washington. I know how it works - you, on my schedule, not me waiting in your office with me on your schedule." The man in a suit, sweating. A sense of his own importance palpable.

Tartus sees the look of withering loathing on the faces of house and clan alike. Their secret societies moved into the light of a mine airshaft.

"No. This was simply more urgent," Tartus slowly replies.

"Then I suppose you don't urgently need to keep your job?" Scasey trying to draw Tartus in.

Finally having had enough, Tartus reponds,"Yes. More important than my job," pronouncing the word with a disgust none of them are used to seeing in him.

"See what you think when none of you have any place to go home to."

"Funny you should put it that way, agent Scasey," Tartus lets this deadly dry humor surface, sardonic echoes from the stone, knowing it will escape Scasey completely. The others, knowing Tartus, realizing he will not take much more. Hardly ever seeing him at this point.

Fenur actually snickering.

"Dunderhead," Hano offers up to Scasey.

Scasey looks at him, momentarily flummoxed.

"Dolt," Hano continues.

"I feel safer already," Tarnus a distant roaring of water under rock.

"I see Fenur - who you don't know - is here." He stops, challenging Tartus, looking at the group.

"It's whom, agent Scasey: Fenur whom we do not know. We notice these things. English is not our first language, and we made a study of it," Tarnus rasps, leaning on a digging implement.

"You think this is funny?" Scasey shouts. A sort of nervousness to him now, as though he realizes something about this group, this moment, the body, is wrong.

Scasey finally focusing on the body, having taken it in before, registering it but not. Looks at Fenur again, registering the katana.

"Who is this?" he bends over from the waist and looks into the vacant countenance of Norvil.

Fenur looks the other way.

Scasey looks up at Fenur. "Have you told them?" He looks at Fenur. Fenur continues to look away.

Scasey begins to laugh.

"Told us what?" Norton asks.

"Has Fenur told you his part in this person's murder?" Scasey finishes.

"What...?" asks Leanor, looking at Fenur, and then pushes it down inside her, closing it off from the local inhabitant.

"No?" Scasey asks Fenur.

Tartus from the corner of Fenur's vision: disappointment.

Something hardening in the shorter one.

Scasey's humor dying. "And you, sir? Where did you find the money to bail out the other mine workers?" Scasey asks Tartus.

"The way I choose to live, is not reflective of my true wealth, Agent Scasey," Tartus says. "You would not understand what it means to dig, or why we do it. My wealth is in my people, and our fraternity. Not in metals, or stones."

Leanor adds,"And our wealth is not in the luxury we enjoy. We have history and blood."

Scasey stunned, trying for a return barb. He defaults back to Fenur, standing close enough for Fenur to feel Scasey's breath and spittle,"You killed him."

"No. I did not. I had thought your kind killed him. For his arrogance and what he didn't understand. And that I had simply stood by."

The group closing around the two. Leanor a complex mix. Tartus disconsolate. Tihan makes a gesture meaning something untranslatable. Refusing to look at Fenur. Norton a quiet rage. "They killed him," he points at Norton, Vilhan and Konor. Leanor turning in shock. Fenur adds softly,"Not that even my friends would have believed me. I stopped them from giving your wife a worse scare." Tartus and the other underpeople stiffening at Fenur's rebuke.

"In fact," Tihan says,"He does not appear wholly dead."

Scasey unable to process what Fenur has said. "My kind...?" He looks at the group – processing. Blinking. "You think this is funny?" Scasey mutters to himself, shaking his head, realizing...

"I see the merits of the joke," Tartus responds without a smile.

Scasey snaps, pushes the far shorter Tartus who stumbles into the other diggers and Fenur. Fenur still standing on Norvil's hand. Knocking Fenur over, surprised.

Scasey with a hand to his weapon, grabbing at the bottle of mead from Tartus's hand.

The body released as Fenur stumbles - are the eyes open, staring unfocused? The mead in freefall.

The body at the wall without movement as Fenur tries to turn himself. The mead continuing the short drop to stone.

"Your concern overwhelms me," Tartus like iron on granite as he scrambles on his knees towards the body, too late. The body of Norvil again moved, a hand on Hano holding the pendant, touching... Light.

Confusion. Uniqueness of vision meeting in a moment.

Hano snatching at the pendant, jerking it away again. Too late.

The temperature drops.

"Get back!" Hano shouts into the chaos, jumping back behind the steering wheel of the roadster, not even bothering to close the door. The others flung backwards, arc lights flying at odd angles, darkness spinning in on them, a brighter point of light where contact has been made.

Bottle breakage, dreams of a homecoming, a place of belonging, rushing in. Being eaten and subsumed into something else.

The arc lights snapping, popping as they hit the carved out walls, Tartus flung into the little electric cart, sound going away in reverberation, pressure change. Hano hitting the pitiful horn which beeps a tinny warning. Scasey propelled up on to the hood of the roadster by a wave of energy from the initial point, denting the hood, appearing to be unconscious where he lays.

Tihan clings to the door of the car pushing herself inside. Behind her the crate of mead. She checks for Tartus and can't see him near the point of contact. She hurls the mead forward past, into the opened portal. Hano with the car already in reverse.

Tartus somehow on his feet, further away than he was, hanging on to Scasey's electric cart which has also been blown a few feet by the breach. The others recovering from the initial wave, pulling themselves on to the cart. Tartus backing up, followed by the vintage roadster.

Momentarily stunned, Fenur recovers. Having missed the cart he jumps onto the hood of the roadster, pinning Scasey there. Scasey coming to for a moment, trying to look up - look into the light...

The roof of the dig disintegrating. Mead bursting into a fireball, shower of flame and rock, a cave-in in front of them squelching down.

Tartus stopping, counting diggers at the point of collapse.

Hano and Tihan out of the still running roadster.

"Nusmo!" Tartus shouts – sound a far away concept after the noise of contact. Blood running into his beard from a gash to his head.

One of the other diggers shaking her head, holding onto Tartus, stopping him before he can start to dig at the point of collapse. The group stumbles trying to get bearings as flashlight torches flicker to life, eyes adjust to the illumination of the roadster's headlamps, and what little light is reflected from further away in the mine through dust.

Fenur raising himself from gray-out - off of Scasey, off the hood of the car.

Tartus already on Scasey before he can recover.

"Tartus," Fenur starts, realizing he is wet. Realizing what the smell of the wetness is. Wet and black in the near complete night.

Bringing a fist down,"You are the liability! You are the dangerous one! YOU KILLED ONE OF MY DIGGERS!"

"Tartus, he has died," Fenur says.

39.


No one pulls Tartus from the man. Tartus realizing what Fenur has said, letting go of the body of Scasey, shocked. The heap that was Scasey, lying in front of the car in the headlights, part of one of the arc lights protruding from his side. "You rude, disrespectful..." Tartus stops. "You were too stupid to explain to."

Others look to the point of collapse where the body of the young one, Nusmo, is momentarily entombed.

"He is with them now," Tarnus chokes out.

Norton looking down at the body of Scasey," Wait..." down on a knee. "I don't think he's dead." He unbuttons the man's shirt. A slight bubbling from the wound made by the sharp length of the arc lamp. "He's breathing. Or crying. The air moves in and out."

"I was tempted to feed him the dark mead, and throw a hammer at him," Tihan suggests. The others look at her, shocked. "What? I was."

"We should put him on the cart," Hano suggests. "I think he should remain flat. He won't fit in the car."

Tartus looks, counting injured. "Injured on the cart," Tartus with the voice of command. "Who made the mead this time? There is no mark of the maker on the bottle. We agreed we would only make it in time of need."

"What greater need than now?" Hano asks.

"Go," Tartus says to uninjured diggers that were helping Tartus restrain the body of Norvil run back towards the entrance. "Off with you then," Tartus says to the backs' of the other diggers sending them into the mine, towards other shafts to find and warn the others.

Tarnus, Hano and Tihan around the body, lifting Scasey, carrying him to one of the triple rows of seats of the electric cart.

Tartus's walkie-talkie coming alive. The pulse of the mine changes, the feel of it returning to them through the stone. "Where are we needed, Tartus?" coming to him again and again over the radio.

"There was a collapse. It is over."

Fenur at his side. Tartus sharply jerks away from him, still stiff at Fenur's upbraiding.

Into the walkie-talkie's mic, Tartus saying,"Everyone evacuate past the seal. As quickly as possible."

Tom, Tartus' boss, from his office, asking from the walkietalkie,"What is happening Tartus? Is there some emergency? Who is here?"

"There is. But there is nothing you can do, Tom."

A pause, then Tom with a slight guffaw over the speaker.

Then,"Why haven't you followed protocols?"

"I am following protocols. I don't know if I can explain."

"You had better, if you don't want me to cancel your orders."

Tartus silent while he keeps himself from snapping at Tom as a king would trying to mentally put into words what is happening so that the man will understand.

Tom on the walkie-talkie. "Everyone hold positions, unless someone has direct knowledge of a containment issue."

Another moment's silence while Tartus fumes. Then Tartus responds,"We haven't ascertained any information about the lab."

"Alright. Continue, I guess. Check the lab for breaches. Any injuries in the cave-in?" Tom again.

Before Tartus can respond on the mic, he hears Morno:"Tartus? We're on our way top side, past the seal."

Rumblings in the mine as diggers move, machinery chatters to a stop. Suddenly, the deep sounds of digging emanating from the earth stop. Under where the reverberations of mine life were, a new lack of sound, and more ominous. Above them diggers making for the outside, trying to remov themselves from harm's way.

Another moment as Tartus gets into the electric cart with the remaining diggers. Examining the body of Scasey, Tartus says in to the walkie-talkie,"Yes There are several casualties."

Finally Tom returns,"Ok. Everyone: listen to Tartus."

Tarnus jamming into the roadster followed by Fenur, crawling of Tihar "Get off me, man!" she protests. Fenur already in behind Hano.

Hano grumbling,"Man..." throws the roadster into reverse, sending more dust up to reflect in the headlamps, hiding the collapse.

Tartus in the cart, whirring away in front of the roadster, which snarls, reverses back through the narrow tunnel of the mine. Hano looks for the path, stretched around in his seat, slightly too short.

Tartus in the electric cart looking back at them, carrying the bodies of the wounded. Of Scasey.

The gloom has deepened around the car and cart as the mine roof has receded. Tarnus in the rear of the roadster with Fenur, Hano and TIhan in front, the rough road jostling the four occupants, following the small electric cart. The infrastructure of the mine around them as the cart and the roadster thread towards the surface.

The seal of the dig in front of them.

The electric cart with the injured and bodies through the seal, followed by the roadster. "Close the seal," Tartus commands and the seal closes.

Tom at Tartus's side. "Nothing's getting through there."

"But what was it?" Tom asks, "What was it?" Turning and looking at Tartus. "Tom, as your friend, leave it to us."

Behind Tartus, Tihan saying, "If Scasey's rash actions destroyed..."

"I know," Tartus waving her off. "The point of crossing could be breached, even now..." Tartus ignoring her, focusing on Tom.

Tom looks at Tartus for a moment, and then walks away out of the mine, hurrying others along.

"Wait!" Tartus says. Tom turns around.

"Can you take this one – agent Scasey - with you?" Tartus asks.

Tom nods. "Let's get the wounded out of here." Tom enlists a few of the locals in moving the body of Scasey.

"Contain the leak," Tom says by way of goodbye.

A bloody trickle from Tartus's scalp.

Tihan at his side, counseling: "They know nothing of what we are like on the inside. You cannot let them evacuate us to a hospital where we can be examined. We will be in the same position as the tall ones were with Norvil."

Even as Tartus makes an affirmative gesture, Tihan is already on her way to find a solution. Tihan looking for a few of the medics from Kragsteeth, and is surprised to find them already making their way towards the injured. Then surprised at her own surprise.

She turns back in time to see Tartus marching toward the great seal where Fenur stands. Tartus next to him.

"What did you say about a laboratory?" asks Fenur.

Tartus doesn't answer, instead looking past the seal at the darkness within the dig.

After a moment Fenur says,"I had to take up with those sorts of locals. I'm the only one of my kin left. I needed allies in this world. I couldn't stay with the underpeople."

Tartus still staring past the seal; into another time.

"Whatever Scasey thought I had done, you were only too willing to believe it. Norvil... would have met with the same end eventually either way. It is a fitting end to his life. Even the last night I saw him; it was the same as always. You're people wouldn't have me. We are too different."

Tartus finally turns and looks up at him, a strange mixture of resignation, anger, pity and grief. "Yes. We are." Tartus walks away.


40.


"Are they through?" asks Morno who directs the other diggers here at the surface.

"We don't know."

Tihan remarks "Maybe what they are... it's what we will be inevitably."

"What do you mean? Fenur asks, looking into the dark as Tarnus holds his arm and hand. Tartus checking it over.

Interrupting this line of thought before it turns fractious, Tartus says,"We are concerned that the way of existence for the houses – we have been dug a similar fate."

Tihan silently agreeing, repulsed by the unpleasant thought. Then she continues, but more politically phrased;"Maybe the well of forgetting is a point that only changes their location in time. Maybe the point of their exit on our side at the well of forgetting became weaker for some reason."

Hano grumbling,"More science thinking-"

Tihan interrupting,"Yes. But the local's have made observations of similar sorts of things in the stars."

Hano asking her,"Wait... ...the silver at our point of crossing attracted us to this world. What is the metal stored in this mine called?"

"Uranium," she offers.

"Maybe it has an even stronger pull on the, the-" "Time rift," she says, using the local term.

"Maybe it has slowly pulled the crossing point to this location from up in the mountains as the stockpiling has occurred. The more - uranium - the more the crossover point moved."

Tihan continues thinking through another aspect,"At the well of forgetting the houses go in, and return in a different time, different; Norton said they don't know what happens at their point of exit. Maybe the chain of events, the disjunction in time, has spread with them - spread the rupture from the point of their exit like a kind of pox."

Hano agreeing,"The spreading rift of this exit point expanding – it explains why the accumulation always must expand. It explains why it could be stopped but not killed, and how we were converted into it: our kind were pushed into the spreading rift – changed along with them. Where ever the accumulation is close together, the pull of the rift is strongest."

"Our kind don't know they're dead?" asks Tarnus.

"No," Hano returns in his blunt way. "And the houses can no longer complete the act of meeting with their own fate." Changing subjects midstream, Hano says,"It was very close for you in the mine, Tartus. The explosion..." Hano scratching fiercely at his beard as he talks; a socially acceptable way of showing his fear.

"I am better. Or nearly. Is my hair singed?" "Does it matter? You have plenty," Tihan offers.

Tartus responds with the completion of Tihan's implied adage,"I am strong." But he takes the welding glasses from his head where they press into his injury.

"If the accumulation is what the tall ones were or will become," Hano says undiplomatically,"Have they made their fate ours?"

Tarnus thinking,"A terrible thing – to think of yourself, or your people in that way."

"Our fate is bound to theirs' now with or without the accumulation," Tartus rumbles.

"It could not be otherwise now," Tarnus meaning the history of the war and the fall; and after, the escape. "We are at the rock's core now."

"If what you posit is true, we cannot let it be known," Tartus looking towards the tall ones, also conferring. An angry council.

Tarnus in agreement. "It would be open war - they would have nothing to lose by staying here. By taking everything of ours' to prevent their own end. Or for that matter what belongs to the locals."

Leanor disengages from the other tall ones, Tartus trying to read their strange body language.

"Do you have any solutions?" she asks.

"No," Tartus says, perfunctorily.

"We do not believe we can wait for the point to pass this location," Hano offers. "If it will," he adds.

"The point?"

"The point of the houses' exit at the well of forgetting. We believe it destabilized. That the accumulation formed because of the destabilization."

"Impossible!" Norton sputters at them.

"And what of home?" Leanor asks, ignoring him.

"It could be gone," Tartus preempts.

"It's like a dream. A game we once played..." Leanor, not prone to reverie, surprising them all with this.

Morno walking back towards them from managing the crowd of miners. Tartus grateful for the help and not having to direct it to be done.

Overhearing, Morno says,"More irresponsible cowardice. What if they have crossed and are even now on their way to the surface? Leave the accumulation here for this world? It is our duty."

Konor returns to Morno,"Duty? You speak to me of duty now in this place? Duty is for home. For a situation where it can be applied. This. Is. Not. That."

"The place does not change what you must be," Morno rejoins.

"We will see-" Norton begins but is cut off by Leanor who says,"Morno is correct. We cannot leave this problem behind for these people. Even if we could fight our way through... No." Leanor still thinking. "Wait for the point to pass... how long?"

Hano growling back,"Let me see... the azimuth is that way... ...and it's been how many years since our arrival...?" Then shouting,"I just said: I don't know!

"It may not pass. It may be the metals in the mine attracting the crossover point away from our original location. We have accumulated a metal here that interacts more strongly with the fissure between our world and this than our silver did."

"And we don't know if the point moved for this reason," Tihan adds. "It could have moved for a reason we have yet to discern."

"Or it could move even deeper into the earth now than it is. In the silver mine at the point of crossing it was nearly on a mountaintop," Tartus ponders. "Then we began working here, at the beginning of the uranium being stored here. But eventually, the rupture could become inaccessible."

"Then entry will also be inaccessible on the other side," Tihan offers.

Tartus grunts a confirmation to what she says. "Maybe."

"Like the song," Tarnus says.

"Almost like it's happened before-" Tihan begins.

"How strong is this seal? " Tarnus asks.

"Not strong enough..." Morno says from further back.

"DO SOMETHING!" Konor shouts.

"What would you have us do that has not been tried?" Hano asks.

Tartus opens another bottle of mead and passes it to the other diggers. Shared libation.

"That is not what I meant," Konor says.

Norton saying,"What can be done...?"

Leanor stepping into the rising panic,"Tartus. Are there explosives? This is a mine afterall."

Tartus, staring at Fenur, is yanked from his reverie,"No. No explosives."

"Father! Your phone! Find out where the others are enroute," Leanor commands.

Norton signals that he understands and begins to make the call.

Tartus glaring at Norton dialing, rereading the sign serving as a reminder bout cell phones.

Norton calling.

"Still nearly an hour," Norton hanging up.

"-The pendants. United with the pendant at the point of crossing-" Hano working through the logic of events, hands on the roof of the roadster. He shouts at Leanor, standing next to him, and at Norton and the rest,"It's a kind of lodestone! The lodestone orients your bodies somehow!" They stare back at him where he leans against the vintage Japanese.

Tihan states for their benefit,"It's a kind of loadstone. Keeping you in time."

Norton taken aback. "Yes. We do not know how it works. When new members of the houses arrive after emerging from the north, we feel them as family. Or we do not. They always find those who remember them. Usually they arrive with a bit of stone they have found from the well of ice. It is made into their pendant by our jewelers. Sometimes they do not arrive with a piece of the stone – it is natural to grab at something that makes one feel better. So it is at the emergence. We have been far to the north – to the lip of the well. We met Morno exploring for new veins in the north, when we were collecting the lodestone we turn into pendants, for those arriving who do not have a stone from the well. Before is... murky."

"Give them to us," Hano says flatly.

The lack of preamble causing Norton to explode. "HAVE YOU LOST ALL REASON!" "The pendants draw the accumulation, and keep the way back open. We believe that is what you will become," Tihan says quietly studying the seal. "Norvil is dead. And you have pushed us into that chasm with you. We may be able to curtail the spreading rift in our lives."

"It may be the only way," Tartus states.

"What will you do? Explode them like some, some-" Leanor trying to think of an appropriate insult.

"No," Hano abrupt, ending the line of querying.

Tihan asks, half-rhetorically,"The depleted uranium separator might be strong enough?" She looks to Tartus and Tarnus. They make a gesture of assent.

"There is no escape from the separation lab," Tarnus reminds her. "If it breaks through - if they are trying to find their way to the surface..."

"It is the best chance," Tartus says. "Perhaps at home-"

Hano makes a gesture of cutting off speculation. Then,"Tell the other ta. ones to stay away. It will dilute the effects of the loadstones you wear a pendants. The rift can be stopped here. If the rift is stopped, the accumulatio will fall. We will collect and destroy the other pendants later. The closer we are together, the more powerful the pendants are."

Over the din of stress Leanor this time, but sounding less sure.

"We will not."

"You – you are animals. Worse. We are evolved!" Norton disgusted. "The pendants keep us from the needs of the world! Look at the Far Sea people – they were beasts. This one soiled one of my own flesh-"

"Needs? Of this world or our own world? I see you as having many needs here. Which even the luxuries you are accustomed to cannot fulfill," Fenur returns starkly.

"Shut your mouth, savage!" Norton slaps him.

The shorter ones agape.

"You don't know that she is your daughter, even if you feel it."

Fenur continues, ignoring the blow. "Us, the less evolved of the Far Sea, understood our relationship with our kindred. And with time."

Vilhan and Norton disgusted, Vilhan saying,"How could you have a craving for this base nature, queen?"

Norton trying to form words, outraged,"It is an abominaton, to not accept those from the north, to not hear the call of the southern lands... it – it is... you-" he splutters.

"Do you not understand that you DISGUST us?" Vilhan roaring at Leanor, at Fenur.

Hano very serious in a way he seldom is. "The pendants are the cause of the disjunction causing the accumulation. They are intricately linked with the point of emergence in the north and of your passing in the south. The rift has been spread by the wearing of the pendants. It is possible we can contain it here with only yours. These three are willing to give their lives for the possibility." Hano realizes something, asks,"What went wrong during your exploration? What was it?"

"Some things are for us only," a venomous statement from Norton.

Morno silent.

Tartus countering,"And if the accumulation is your future? If that is what lies in the south? Is that what you desire?" Tartus looks back towards the seal. "You can stop that future and destroy them."

"You think-" Leanor counters, then shudders to a stop. "It has been in my thoughts," finally admitting a terrible thing.

The fury of Norton, Vilhan and Konor. Morno at a distance from his own kind and the taller ones.

Hano, unusually for him, quieter, conceding,"It is the only thing left. We all are growing weaker, the nature of what we are recedes – we are becoming more like the locals. It is only a matter of time. Why not embrace what must be?"

"No," Norton says, radiating a brutal kind of prejudice at Fenur and the clans. "I won't allow it. It is what we are." The group startled to silence at this outburst in front of the queen.

A moment, then,"You will not allow it?" Leanor asking icily.

Norton continuing on, haughty,"Someone has to protect what has always been. Your actions as queen have been abominable. To give yourself – your body and essence – to some animal. If only I had-"

"Protect what has always been? Is that what you call what you did to Norvil?" Fenur asks.

Tartus - sensing a moment is passing - lobs into this,"They asked me to plot your assassination with Fenur, queen."

Shocked silence.

The slither of katana.

Norton, hearing the sound, turns to look at Fenur, as the blade

Leanor has quickly drawn from its sheath on Fenur's back strikes Norton down. A sharp spike in Norton's pendant light, followed by a sudden dimming.

"FENUR, NO-" Tartus shouts, Fenur looking confused. The group realizing Leanor holds the sword, already kicking the mid-torso of Norton's body to free it, and whirling on Konor.

"I AM THE QUEEN! YOU KNEW OF THIS?" a near shriek in the old language. Konor falling back in terror, looking for escape and slipping in Norton's blood. On his knees he begins to scurry away. Leanor skewering him as he crawls.

"This is not what I intended!" Tartus trying to stop her but the sharp blade limits reach in the confined space of digging implements, keeping the shorter ones away.

"DO NOT-" Tartus commands in the brackish tongue of his clan.

Stepping over the two bodies, Leanor advances on Vilhan.

"Leanor-" Vilhan begins.

"How could you not have known of this plot?" Leanor asking Vilhan sharply.

"I-"

Leanor stops in her advance on Vilhan. Sinks against earthmoving equipment, her reserves cracking, or thinking better of severing the tie of her house and her husband's.

Fenur cuffs Morno across the neck with a hand, the last member of the conspiracy, and with a last look at the shorter one, shoves him towards his people.

Leanor stopped, her back to the earthmoving equipment, suddenly composed again, examining Morno and Vilhan – insect like in her gaze. The sword across her lap, suit bloodied, dirty. Leanor breathing heavily.

Tihan looks away from the ugliness.

Tartus and Tarnus ignoring the pleading from Morno.

Tartus steels himself for the total breakdown between clan and house.

Fenur spits,"It is what you ask of me. All of you. Always." He looks to Leanor. "She had no choice. I understand this. Do not judge for what you have not the will to do," he chokes out, taking the blade back from her and cleaning it on his suit jacket.

Tartus visually checking the seal, avoiding what is in front of him by being distant, thinking: regret? inevitability?.

Leanor rising, leaning back, sick. "Father..." Also in the old language.

Into this Morno whispering,"I will return to the ranks."

No one stops him. Vilhan following "Wait." Leanor commanding,"Remove his pendant." Vilhan stops, trembling.

Fenur stepping in close to him, Fenur's hand on the place where the pendant hangs from Vilhan's neck, stopping it from swinging. Fenur pulls it free, snapping the necklace. Leanor's husband publicly shamed. Fenur places Vilhan's pendant in Leanor's hand.

"Take the pendants from the others," Hano commands in a low voice. "We don't know how much time there is. Leanor, give us yours."

Slowly, Leanor accedes, unfastens the pendant from her neck.

Tihan reaches down and gathers the two pendants from the pools of blood. Taking Leanor's last.

Tartus finally saying,"You know I could not allow you to kill Vilhan, Leanor. Or one of my own kind. It would be total war among the houses. A political marriage cannot be undone by blood. Not without even more. You will see it in time."

Leanor makes a motion meaning agreement.

Tartus says,"Hano. The car."

"This time I will go as well," Leanor adds, rising from her place where metal meets stone.

41.

"There can't be much time-" Tarnus looking away into the dark of the mine.

"Will you come with us?" Tartus asks Fenur. "In truth, your burden is lifted."

"It would be wrong for me not to take the burden of all the houses and carry it to its end," Fenur says. "Maybe I can make amends."

Tartus suppressing whatever complicated thing he would like to say to the boy.

"We take the roadster, drive it down to the depleted uranium lab?" Fenur asks.

"Yes," Hano affirms.

"Enough. Leanor, Fenur, Tarnus and Tihan, with me. Hano – you will stay. Escape if you must. Contact the locals if all else fails. Make them listen. Be our envoy. We need Tarnus for the lab. Otherwise as court consul he would stay with you." Hano with an affirmative gesture of farewell.

Tartus behind the wheel of the roadster.

Hano saying,"I love that car. I know it's not going to make it out of here." Leanor and Fenur crawling into the back, their lengths balled up.

"If we do not return. Hold an election. As the locals would."

He closes the car door. "We have seen what kings purchase us," Tartus adds, the window still down on the passenger side.

Hano says,"I will do as you ask. I do not know if the locals or our own kind will listen."

"Let us hope," Tartus returns. Tarnus, Tihan, Leanor and Fenur arranging themselves. The two diggers twisting next to Tartus, uncomfortable in the cramped front seat. Tartus turns the ignition and the roadster squirms, trying to find purchase on the cold rock.

Morno opens the seal.

They shoot through - the rough ride of suspension, blurring, crane housings and support structures.

Smoke rises from below, smell of burning diesel fuel and rubber - damage from the dark mead, and wrecked equipment. A choking soot from a black orifice emanating palpable dread which gives chase.

The back end of the roadster breaks free at the turn towards the lab, sliding before scrappling back into forward momentum.

A second turn, Tartus searching for gearing. Thoughts of the accumulation emerging from the dark hole in the earth.

Slalom among more storage crates.

"You know the other option is," Tartus contemplates as they descend,"that we're about to give the accumulation access to the hardest substance we've found."

"Would the accumulation know what to with the depleted uranium?" Tarnus musing.

"Battering rams at Kragsteeth," Fenur says.

After the jarring shock of the homemade bomb, Leanor's rage, the cool wind through the open windows of the car is eerie. Thoughts of an exterior thing trying to tear a hole in the life they have made. As they approach the bottom branching of the mine, Tartus guns the engine, checking the dash instruments. "He could have put gas in the car. We're nearly empty."

Tartus in first gear again and getting up to speed.

The uranium depletion lab tunnels. The tiny sports car happy for the grip of pavement in the military part of the complex. Tartus redlining the engine into the depleted uranium storage area, sudden change of direction, weight shift, round loading carts, extra bits of the cogwheel train, tooling areas, the stacks of the depleted uranium rods.

It feels as though something is chasing them. Something worse than Scasey, the weight of their own damaged lives, what Leanor has done, what her people had proposed.

Rising panic - something... They can feel the choking breath of it through the dark.

"Hold on," Tartus growls through gritted teeth and the others struggle to hear him. Empty space, off the loading dock, knocking the tool carts out of the way. Lunging for the bottom. Crashing through from the negative space of free flight, heads hitting the headliner, Tihan free in the middle taking the worst bashing. Already bleeding from an ear after the explosion went off so close to them. Covered in glass. The cog track for moving the uranium below chewing through the tires, braking the suspension, one of the rear wheels now working, sending the car careening up and over one of the tracks into the tunnel wall, sparks, Tartus struggling with the steering, guiding the limping car down the steep incline towards the depletion lab, lightheaded as they fall down the ladder-like track. Tihan recovering from having the wind knocked out of her. Tartus's head bleeding again. Tarnus holding one of his hands in the other. Fenur checking on Leanor, sick from the loss of the pendant.

"I can feel them coming," Fenur somehow unscathed looks behind.

Ahead a cograil car stopped on the tracks. Tartus makes a judgement decides to try and squeeze between it and the wall. The cograil car substantial looming, as Tartus aims for the tiny passage to one side. The passenger fender rolling up and taken off by the cograil car as the roadster makes the squeeze through – shrapnel - the fender whirring by close enough to shave Tarnus beard, flipped up onto the walkway next to the cograil. The roadster still being propelled downwards by gravity, Tartus's force of will and fear of what they feel growing behind them.

"Hano's going to bury you down here for that," Tihan tries for composure.

Tartus grunts. The bottom. The airlock for the rail system.

The five unfolding from the interior of the car as quickly as possible, Tartus springing forward, keying the door of the leaded airlock.

The large door opens, sliding sideways. Inside, Tartus re-keys as everyone looks back up the tunnel. Behind them clanks, cracklings – the settling of broken equipment. They see nothing behind. And yet...

"All this security, military even, and they evacuate at the first sign of trouble. The locals are weak," Tarnus; the mullings of quiet thunder.

On the interior of the airlock, an unloading dock, tools for working on the cog cars. Carts for moving the heavy rods. Forklifts.

"How do you fight this thing they bury here?" Leanor wonders, an opposing view. "I'm sorry - I must keep talking - it helps me focus." She leans on Fenur. "I haven't removed my pendant in... I don't remember when."

"The radiation? Then why militarize it at all? They are fools." Even as they talk, waiting for the door, they move back towards the far wall. Tarnus ready at the lock for the interior airlock.

The keypad where Tarnus stands accepts his input. The interior door begins to slide open. Stops. The fear. The choking darkness. Tartus slides the axe from his long coat, prying at the remaining gap.

Leanor hobbling through braced by Fenur. Not unscathed – she's having trouble putting her foot down. Expensive shoes gone, barefoot in the lab.

Inside, the sound of the pulverizer and compactifier missing from the normal mix of the depletion process. The lab darker than usual. Emergency lighting. The inner airlock door closing behind them, cutting off the dread momentarily.

"We must restart the pulverizer." Tartus says. "Tihan; the computers and monitoring system. Through the floor they hear something working at the airlock and the smaller door above which lies at the end of the walkway running parallel to the cograil track. Tartus double checks the military desk above, running up a flight of stairs to look back at the small interior antechamber through the armored leaded glass of an observation window. Again the fear begins to consume them. The desk where a military official sits vacated. Paperwork spread haphazardly across the desk. "As I thought," Tartus says to the state of the paperwork.

The anteroom built over the cograil airlock, its own smaller entry and airlock system. Tartus tries to remember if even he has ever been on this side of the lab's large armored window or if he has always been outside, accepting a verbal check from the scientists within, and collecting paperwork from the military official. "The tools of wars, secreted away out of sight. Responsibility put on us. Cowards." He makes a mental note. Besides the abandoned military desk he sees that the door to the smaller antechamber airlock - it seems about to fail.

"Fenur, Leanor – how will your kind react to radiation?" Leanor waves the question off, sick at losing the pendant.

"Pulverizer coming online," Tihan checks in from a bank of computers at the rear of the lab.

"Are the cryo-separators working? Are the lines open from the pulverizer?" Tartus back down on the raised grid flooring – a system that allows scientists access to the piping system that flows to cryo-separator tubes while still being able to walk around, the guts of the system under them – raise a metal mesh grating, drop down to the tubing, make adjustments, check pressures, make fixes among the lead piping. The actual separators rising through square holes in the grating, pushing upwards into the gloom above, like missiles frozen in place. Along the sides of the separator tubes are various hatches allowing ingress to the internals of the cryo process. The processing, or freezing, of the two different atomic weights of the isotopes of uranium cause them to come to rest in the bath of liquid nitrogen at various pre-prescribed heights along the lengths of the tubes. Ladders up the sides of the tubes for accessing the hatches containing the valve systems which create the shunts moving the isotopes from the tubes after purification over to the compactifier. Other shunts for the small amounts of offal in the system.

Tartus following along the pipes, looking down through the metal mesh flooring, looking for problems with the separators, anything that would keep the pendants from leaving the pulverizer.

"The cryotubes can only be put into a low power mode, but there wasn't time at the evacuation..." The bright lights of the lab kick back on as the system comes online. "It's ready," Tihan says.

"Tarnus - the pendants," Tartus commands.

"Tartus, are you sure? I would be remiss if I did not point out that this could mean open war here."

"We are sure," Leanor chokes out. "If just these five pendants are enough to pull them towards us and away from the surface. Imagine if the houses had arrived before... Certainly so many pendants so close to the crossing point – it would have broken open. There is no other way." Leanor collapsing into Fenur. "DO IT!"

Tarnus at the rear of the lab next to a large apparatus. A giant piston in a lead housing, a radiation seal hatch and a conveyor belt behind it. The piston as smasher. After the pulverizer atomizes the particulate it is ground down further by a series of finer and finer gratings, finally falling into a solution of frozen nitrogen, flows, makes its way through a series of pipings to the cryotubes rising through the center of the lab. The thumping they associate with the lab begins as Tihan brings the lab fully online, and the pulverizer is activated.

Terror sweeping them up. The world darkening.

Tarnus places the pendants on the conveyor belt behind the radiation hatch where normally the uranium ore would be placed. Ready to return them to their component elements. Tarnus looking at Tartus, then Leanor and Fenur.

Fenur says,"It is the only way. After, we will have to gather the remaining pendants." Tarnus closes the hatch, saying,"It will be civil war."

"Perhaps." Leanor insensate at the loss.

Tartus watching the system. The calm against the panic eerie.

Tihan says,"I only hope there is enough room in the cryotubes for the offal. In theory they can hold large amounts, although the uranium ore is fairly refined when it arrives and should not contain much other material. A processing was a little more than half complete, but the uranium is out of the system now. The pendants should be only offal - but we've never tested them - we don't know what they're made out of. The cryotubes will separate them out into their component parts. We can just turn the system off when it is complete-" Tihan jumps as the window above collapses inwards, the smaller airlock door from the airlock above hitting and shattering it. The emergency lighting flickering. Pressure.

"Protect the lab!" Tartus commands.

Tartus up the stairs, with his axe. The bottleneck of the small antechamber.

Tihan with a wrench stands fast at the rows of computer banks, poised for an advance. Leanor pulling herself from the floor, seizes on a fire extinguisher, using its weight to stand. Nausea and pain.

"Tartus...!" Tihan's voice rising to near panic as the skin of a cryotube cracks. A plume of frozen nitrogen vapor boiling off from a tube puncture. The piston and sieve system working harder, deliberating over each crushing blow, each atom of pendant pushed into the system. Mist. More punctures. More nitrogen vapor - swell of something wrong - something, a feeling, trying to retrieve the pendants. Near white out from the overhead lighting, shadows deranged in the emergency lighting. The nitrogen mist pumping blindness and panic into the room.

"Protect Tihan! Protect the apparatus!" Tartus shouting.

Leanor lost in the mist as another tube is punctured. Lights going out. Alarms. Radiation leak alarms.

Fenur through the mist, sword raised, finds himself face to face through the fog with Norvil.

"See what you are capable of?" quiet words from Norvil in the cacophony. "You have destroyed our family. You have killed whole races, erased ancestries, of your own people and now others. Why deny yourself what you really desire? Lead us."

Saying nothing, Fenur strikes at Norvil through the mist, missing Norvil in a lunge, off-balance, a swarm of what seems like others behind, hidden in the nitrogen fog.

Tarnus still making noise from above. The noise of the smasher a thronging. Scraping and expectorations.

Fenur screaming in the dialect of his people. The hallucination of Norvil.

Flashing alarm lights. Yellow. Suddenly red.

Tartus through the chaos working his way back to the pulverizer and the banks of computers, fearing what he will find. The gash on his head, and the blood running again, blinding him in one eye. Wind knocked from him by the chaos.

A glimpse of something below on the cement floor next to the cryo-piping where the ore, or pendants, enters the tubes for collection. Tarnus. Not moving. A hand on the support structure for the cryotube. Tarnus lifting himself up, looks up at Tartus - registering. A gesture for good health, too tired to speak.

Tartus searching through the cool nitrogen fog and alarms.

The lifting of fear.

"Tihan? Fenur? Leanor?" Shouting, barely able to see.

Tihan emerging through the mist with Leanor.

Realization. "FENUR!"

Another moment, Tartus finding strength to run in the direction he last saw the boy.

"Fenur!"

"Here." Fenur, holding his side. "I'm here." "We have to go," Tihan prompts. "The separation is complete. We have no idea how we will respond to any radiation. Or the others," meaning Fenur and Leanor. Her beard covering a darkening bruise seen even in the half-light and alarms.

The five make their way up the stairs and out of the lab, to the smaller airlock in the antechamber above the cograil. Climbing out of the lab onto the gantry, over the wrecked car on the cograil below. A feeling, a sense of acridity, a syrup of hysteria dissipating from where it flooded the little antechamber access point to the separation lab. Ghastly remains of their shared histories. Past, finally out of the silent tomblike tunnel, finding footing, moving as quickly as possible towards the surface.

42.

One of the diggers at a set of controls on the outside; the seal turning on its axis, chatter of broken bearings and deep earth groan, giving out during the final bit of pressure weighing down, the seal pie-slice of a door arriving at ground level, opening for them to walk through.

Hano at the other side of the seal to meet them as they emerge.

"Should we check for the opening at the bottom of the dig?" Tartus asks Hano as they step through.

"No need – as soon as the pendants were destroyed, we could feel the rift nap back." Hano adds,"But check if you want to to."

Tartus dispatches someone.

"Where did...?" Fenur prods.

"Norton and Konor?" Hano responding,"Morno and a few others came for me after you entered the tunnels. We threw Norton's body from the upper railing. The damage should hide Leanor's sword work. It began again immediately." Hano continues,"Vilhan left in the hotel's helicopter. As did Tom Talius with Agent Scasey in the helicopter Scasey arrived in," Hano says. "We do not know if Scasey will live. I believe Vilhan was in contact with others of the houses before they took off."

Leanor looking concerned, says,"I will deal with it in time.

Vilhan... it was shrewd of my father; our joining. But perhaps shrewd and quick-witted are not the same." She laughs bitterly. "He considered himself a master of politics. My father always thought he was more astute than he actually was." She pauses. "I hope that Vilhan may be convinced that destroying the pendants was the only hope we have."

"In my experience people usually see reason eventually," Tartus observes.

"Many had said the joining would end in blood," Fenur adding to the weight and the tally.

The air clearer on the exterior of the seal.

Leanor with the burden of the patricide, saying weakly,"He did it to avoid blood – I doubt even those who believed it would end this way thought it would be his blood. Tartus, perhaps you are right: I should try to salvage my house's alignment with Vilhan."

Fenur impassive. The shorter ones avoid this awkwardness.

Hano says,"Where's my car?" Tartus points back though the seal.

"You owe me a car!"


43.


Tartus gives a local type shrug, full of irony.

Outside, the diggers, exhausted from the ordeal, sit against equipment or on the ground, against the support structure for the overhead tram, or the railings for the cranes and trains. Seeing the small returning party they begin to stand.

"You return!" "The clans and houses are victorious!"

"The king is alive!"

Word spreading back through the ranks closing around them, touching them, offering congratulations. Shaking the hands of the queen of Nor and the king of Tar alike. Hearty back slaps for the taller ones. Fenur applauded by even the most skeptical of the clans.

Diggers with medical expertise seeing to the gash in Tartus' head, Tarnus broken hand and Tihan's ear and face.

The group making their way from the dig area towards helipads and parking lots, following the tramline out through the stratums of dig organization.

Despite the exuberance of the moment, Fenur turns, asking Tartus,"And what of the other pendants?" Leanor under the relief, still destroyed.

"It is a problem for the queen. Not you. Enjoy the moment," Tartus returns, trying to hide his disillusionment with himself. His view of the boy warped by Fenur's actions at the pass so long ago.

Leanor interjecting,"We will keep the members of the houses as far apart as we can until the pendants can be collected. Keeping the field the pendants create weak." She asks Tihan,"Will that keep the accumulation from rising once more?"

Tihan looking around the hands working on her face,"It should." Hano concurs.

Fenur rejoining the clans excitement. Ale appears, a cooler from the back of a van in the parking lot, and food. A few treats from home.

The lights of the parking area, and a cool desert breeze from the late night air.

Even Leanor accepting an ale, wielding it badly. Rounds of toasts. "The houses and clans!" The names of fallen cities and friends. The names of places long buried and unspoken of.

Fenur smiling but far away as he watches Tartus, Tarnus and Tihan and the others united. Supporting a sagging Leanor.

The person Tartus sent to inspect the place of contact returns. "It is closed," they inform him. Tartus circumspect, not wanting to destroy the jubilant mood.

Sirens and cars. Fire trucks and ambulances hiking in from Vegas. A few dark green vehicles – the locals' coding for military.

"Tim!" Tartus shouts, grabbing the flight specialist from the helipad by the shoulder, bringing him through the madness of the impromptu party. "Tartus, I know there hasn't been a leak - but there are protocols... what was that...?"

Tartus waving it away, using his relief to put Tim at ease after the eldritch happenings, nodding like a local,"I understand, I understand," dismissing Tim's misgivings as part of the night. The shorter ones crowding out the local in the festivities.

Tim called over to the helipad to oversee a lifeflight landing.

"Is someone actually hurt?" Tihan asks, looking at the red helicopter landing, helipad lights throwing emergency insignia into relief, as one of the mine medical officers shaves part of her beard to drain the bruise.

"Protocol," Tartus returns, offhandedly. Another medical officer dabbing his head with stinging alum. "And Scasey..."

Tartus leans into Leanor, the sharp pain from the alum, a truncheon slamming home on a spike, subsiding. "We will begin making the oil again ...somehow. It should ease the, the ...disjunction."

"Yes. Let us hope," Leanor says in return. Still seeming ill.

Hano blustering his way into this, adding,"There are two mages now–" he looks to Tihan, beard half-shaved "-we will find a way; we have traded for centuries. Our devices have been destroyed, but we will make new ones. We will find a way to help the houses orient in time."

"And if we begin to age and die?" Leanor asks.

"Certainly anything must be better than what would have been in the accumulation," Fenur says, listening in.

"We are in it together – we have no dark mead!" Tartus says.

"Agreed. We will find a way," Leanor says. "Once the houses produced it and traded it to the clans. Maybe we could again."

Cessation of sirens and confusion of the emergency personnel as they step from firetrucks and ambulances to find an impromptu party. The military needlessly forming up.

"Some day we will return home," Tartus asserts. "But not today."

Arriving with the teams of EMTs, fireman, police, military from nearby bases, are members of the houses, stopping amongst the larger vehicles, setting foot onto pavement and walking into the festivities, tallest amongst the throng.

Confusion, followed by the narration of events from members of the clans. Some stunned, or angry. Others visibly sagging with relief. Eventually, cell phones opening to stop more from arriving.

Emergency workers pushing through the carousing looking for someone in charge and an explanation.

Tarnus says to the other two,"We still have to get my axe back."

# About the Author

Jay Wright's work has been published with more than a dozen literary presses including Windriver Press's The Paumanok Review, Tachyon, Alternate Realities, Curve, Left Curve with readings at City Lights Bookstore, Cherry Bleeds and Duct Tape Press. He has also worked with Aardman and contributed to the Star Trek franchise, as well as several bestselling video games. His films and videos have appeared in the Biennial of Poetry and Video MUNAL. They are carried by Museo de Nacional in Mexico, the Vatican Contemporary, NMAC Montenmedio Arte Contemporaneo in Spain, MAMAC Nice, Musée d'Art Contemporain de Lyon, PS1 in New York and the Pompidou. His first novel King of Siam was published by Duct Tape Press. Invisible City, another novel which explores themes first presented in King of Siam was orphaned by Doubleday, but has found new life in the digital world. Exiles was attached to Bantam but was not published by them. He has been nominated for a Guggenheim and invited to Arsenal at the Berlin Film Festival and also to the Canary Islands and Florence Biennials, and won several best fest awards at film festivals. His films have also appeared at Cannes Short Film Corner and Clermont-Ferrand. His education includes UC Berkeley, and

a BFA from San Francisco Art Institute where he worked with members of
Cinema 16 and Warhol's Factory.
Read more at https://instagram.conm/assemblerfilms.

Ingram Content Group UK Ltd.
Milton Keynes UK
UKHW022016090323
418309UK00015B/1003